LIFELI

BOOK 1 OF THE LIFELIGHT SERIES

ALINA VOYCE

Published by Lifelight Publishing 2012
Printed and bound by Lightning Source
Designed by Grainger Graphics

www.alinavoyce.com

This book is a work of fiction. Names, characters, businesses, organisations, places, events are the product of the author's imagination or are used fictitiously. Any resemblance to actual persons, living or dead, events or locales is entirely coincidental.

ISBN: 978-0-9571817-0-0

This book is dedicated to Phil, Amy, Stephen and the members of the R.C. (past and present).

With heartfelt thanks for your love, support, patience and the occasional 'talking to' – administered as necessary.

Love y'all.

LIFELIGHTS

CHAPTER 1

Caught by the breeze from the open window, the crystal ornament twisted. Prismatic flashes of sunlight dispersed across walls and ceiling. Mara Austin watched them, fascinated, as she turned out the last of the cakes. The colours were vibrant, almost alive, mimicking the crystal's movements.

Jennie, the owner of The Tea Cosy café and Mara's boss, backed through the kitchen doorway carrying a tray of fresh bread and sandwich fillings. She looked as cool and clean as Mara felt hot and sticky.

She paused, drawing in a deep breath before winking at Mara. The scents of baked sugar, vanilla and cocoa still clouded the oven-warmed air.

"Hmm smells good, darling," she said.

Mara grinned at her. Jennie made working at The Tea Cosy a pleasure, her genuine interest in people and her near encyclopaedic knowledge of her historic home town, Beverton, created a unique atmosphere. Ever friendly, she easily persuaded the café's customers to sit a while, eat more than they intended and, most importantly, keep coming back. Business was booming and Mara wondered if the owners of the franchise coffee shops, in the centre of town, knew what they were missing.

"Yep, won't argue with you there; but you're still not getting any samples," she replied.

"Aw, come on, not even a jam tart?" Jennie said, sticking out her bottom lip.

"Definitely not. I take my role as diet defender seriously, and anyway, you're enough of a tart as it is without adding to the problem."

"I can't believe you said that. Where's the respect?" Jennie gave Mara her best 'puppy dog' look.

Snorting, she rolled her eyes. Jennie never failed to try it on, pouting and cajoling, in an attempt to snaffle a still-warm treat before their customers got to them. Mara knew she was lucky to be working here, away from the overcrowded high street, even if her boss and friend did suffer from occasional bouts of stress related temper and treated personal barriers as minor inconveniences, to be crushed at the earliest opportunity.

Turning the door sign to 'open' the two of them were soon rushed off their feet, as the demand for full English breakfasts flowed seamlessly into orders for morning coffee. The café's till calculated the bill totals with satisfying regularity, even if Jennie did reckon it'd be quicker for Mara to do it herself.

She had a point. For some reason, Mathematics came easily to Mara. If she'd had the confidence, she'd have loved to explore that side of her character further. Numbers weren't just symbols to her. She actually enjoyed working with them… something that Jennie maintained was 'weird'. Girls, apparently, were meant to like shopping, not number crunching.

It was 10:30 before the first break of the day arrived, a chance for them to sit across from each other and catch up. Jennie constantly chatted as Mara listened in silent admiration. The last four years had lowered her defences, but she doubted she'd ever drive a conversation with the same enthusiasm as Jennie.

It was difficult to tell, but she supposed that her friend was about ten years older than her. Far taller than her own vertically challenged stature, Jennie possessed a natural, slender beauty. Not that she exploited this. Her elegant features were showcased with minimal make-up and a simple ponytail. She exuded the sort of confidence that only comes with age and to top it all, had an innate thoughtfulness that never failed to surprise, especially now. Reaching under the table Jennie drew out a long, brightly wrapped present and an envelope, pushing them across to Mara, meeting her look of shock with a sly smile.

"I've told you before; I've got a good memory. Bet you thought you'd got away with it didn't you?" Jennie said, "Happy Birthday, Mara."

Mara continued to stare at the present, blinking back tears. She should have expected this. She always did remember.

"Go on then, open it. I'll let you save the card for later, but don't do what you usually do with presents and stare at it for ten minutes. We don't have time this morning." Jennie teased, "After all, Tommy Tourist will be back before you know it and Pious Pete and the rest of the Church council are booked in for lunch."

After struggling with the tightly knotted ribbon, Mara carefully peeled back the wrapping paper to reveal a necklace, nestled within layers of tissue. It was something she would have picked for herself.

"Oh Jennie, it's beautiful," she said.

"I thought so," Jennie agreed. "Come on, let me put it on for you and see what it looks like. I thought it was perfect for your colouring."

The necklace scintillated against Mara's pale skin as Jennie fastened it in place. She strained her neck, eager to catch her reflection in the mirror across the room.

Sparkling blue beads, in varying shades, were strung onto a darker blue cord. They picked up her eye colour exactly and brought out the blue tones of her thick black hair.

"Thank you Jennie," she said. Their hug felt somewhat awkward but meant as much as the gift.

The moment ended as the café door opened. Jennie went to get an order pad, leaving Mara to clear up their break-time debris. A man walked in, tall and lean, with dark brown hair. One glance told Mara that he was business class rather than tourist, the perfectly tailored suit being the biggest giveaway. For a moment she thought she recognised him; maybe she'd seen him around town? Picking up the tray she made her way back to the kitchen.

"Did you see that gorgeous man?" Jennie said, fanning herself with their customer's order slip as she came back through, "I didn't think they made them like that anymore. He's enough to make my knees go weak," she giggled.

"No, can't say I did," Mara said. "But then, I didn't get a good look at him; I was too busy clearing up. I don't think I've ever met a man who weakens my knees." She paused to give it serious thought. "Well, unless you count that time Grandad came back from the loo without checking he was decent; that made me weak kneed, not to mention nauseous. I was waking up in a cold sweat for months."

Jennie looked stunned, "Err, too much information Mara. Don't forget I knew your Grandad and that mental picture you've given me is just... wrong." She shivered. "Post-traumatic stress disorder still doesn't let you off the hook and you really have to see this one for yourself. You, darling, can take his order out."

"Ha, you're only saying that so it gives you time to touch up your makeup. Fancy your chances with this one do you?" Mara retreated as Jennie threatened her with a tea towel, "Hey! No need to get violent, I'll do it. But I warn you now, men in general don't impress me," Mara smirked, as she took the tray that Jennie held out. She knew it was pointless to argue, and anyway, she was curious.

Expertly balancing the tray in one hand, she carefully placed the tea and cake in front of their customer. She felt uncomfortable, as if he knew exactly what she was doing. She couldn't get a good look at him either. His face was angled away from her, bent towards the newspaper he was reading. 'The Times', it made sense with a suit like that. The photo on the front page caught her attention, it showed a wind turbine; something she'd always thought of as elegant, architecturally speaking. According to the headline, petrol prices were on the up again. What that had to do with the picture she wasn't sure; unless, of course, they'd managed to invent a car that ran on thin air.

The man barely acknowledged her presence and her pathetic attempt to ogle him wasn't helped by her vision blurring over, her eyes burning slightly. All she could see was an out-of-focus face that seemed to shift around oddly in front of her.

Thankfully the irritation was fleeting, all thought of their new customer disappearing as the lunch time rush began.

* * * *

Locking the door of The Tea Cosy, Mara turned to wave at Jennie as she drove past. Glancing at her watch she cursed under her breath; late again.

At this time of day, Beverton's tourists had long since abandoned the Minster and the rest of the town's medieval treasures; leaving the streets unusually quiet. Except for the clamour of Mara's ride home. Breaking into a run, she tore along the pavement, slipping on cobblestones worn smooth over the years.

No matter how close the bus stop, the timing was all too easy to misjudge. Thank God the bus was such a relic, announcing its approach with plumes of black smoke, followed by the occasional cough from its exhaust; otherwise she'd easily miss it, frequently.

The bus driver greeted her in the same way he'd done for the last four years, his mood ever cheerful and infectious.

"Good evening pretty girl. Work okay today?" He asked.

"Yes thank you Mr. Thompson. Yours too?"

A rotund man, who appeared well past retirement age, he shrugged, giving a noncommittal grunt as he took her fare. "It ain't over yet." He said.

Mara took a seat. Tired muscles relaxed against the worn fabric. Leaning her head against the cool glass of the window, she stared out.

The white sign that read 'Thank you for visiting Beverton' passed by, suburbia giving way to Mother Nature. Even in the dim evening light, the beauty of the Yorkshire Wolds was indisputable. Misty, chalk strewn fields, an artist's dream, hedgerows crisscrossing the landscape, adding to the impression of a giant patchwork quilt. The bus' racket faded into nothing more than background noise, the journey morphing into an oasis of calm, a precursor to the comforts of home.

* * * *

It was already 7pm. Mara dawdled up the driveway to her cottage, admiring the sunset. Trees in the near distance were silhouetted against swathes of pink, orange and turquoise blue. Their darkened, leafless branches reminded her of lead, spread out across a glowing stained glass window.

Once through the front door, she kicked off her shoes, leaving them where they fell as she turned to lock out the world. She didn't bother with the lights as she hung up her coat, and anyway, the Lifelights would arrive in a moment, flying towards her from every corner of the cottage.

The darkness was transformed with effervescent light, as vivid balls of energy, about the size of a two pence piece, moved towards her. Always in groups of four, red, blue, green, silver or gold, their colours glowed. They teased her with gentle, heated touches, fizzing against her skin, re-energising weary nerves. Arms outstretched, love swelled inside her as the minutes slipped by. It felt so good to be home. Bending, Mara retrieved the carrier bag that Jennie had given her and headed into the kitchen, the Lifelights beside her. It was on days like this, special days, that she was most thankful for their presence. They were the closest thing to a family she had.

Jennie had excelled herself. The bag contained red wine, homemade lasagne, a green salad and a chocolate cake; complete with fudge icing. A candle and the number 22, marked out in white chocolate drops, adorned the top. Delicious.

Tears once again threatened, even as Mara smiled. She touched the necklace that she'd refused to take off. Jennie had spoiled her. Lighting the candle, she made the customary wish as she blew it out again and went to put her feet up. The Lifelights fussed, arranging themselves around her, along the arms and the back of the sofa. Some nudged at her hands, pushing them aside so they could nestle in her lap.

"You're persistent tonight, aren't you?" She whispered, reaching for the envelope Jennie had given her earlier. She expected the usual bawdy card, deliberately picked, in the hope of causing maximum embarrassment or perhaps a hastily smothered, wicked laugh.

A moment later pain sliced across her right index finger. Mara cursed. Paper cuts stung far more than their size warranted; instinctively, she sucked on the wound.

"Mara." She heard the man's voice clearly. It sounded urgent.

Freezing, her heart raced with sudden fear, her gaze darting to every corner of the room.

"Mara... you're hurt." The voice wasn't going to be ignored.

The Lifelights shifted now, their lights flickering, as if they too could hear it. Mara sat bolt upright, looking around the room, as long moments stretched out. She knew there was no one there though; she could hear where the voice came from. It was in her head.

"Answer me, Mara."

Were the Lifelights finally communicating with her? The idea kicked Mara's pulse rate higher, adrenaline spiking, as shivers of excitement raced along her spine. It has to be she thought, at last.

Closing her eyes for a moment, she drew in a slow, steadying breath, before focusing her attention on the Lifelights again. Their movements appeared unusually graceless, their colours flashing. They'd never behaved like this before.

"I'm fine thank you. It's a small cut. It will soon heal." She said, trying to swallow saliva that wasn't there. She held her finger up to study the paper cut, pretending that she didn't feel silly, talking to herself. "Who are you?" She asked, perhaps too casually, all things considered.

"A friend," the pitch of the voice was lower, definitely friendlier.

"I don't have friends," Mara whispered, before she could stop herself.

"Oh, I think you do. You just haven't opened your eyes to them yet," the voice replied.

It sounded amused, she thought, aware of an indistinct accent, but it was more than just a voice; she could feel it. His words, layered with a confusing mass of emotion, brushed against her mind, and her skin tingled, as if responding to a physical touch.

"What do you mean?" She asked, not knowing what else to do. She was aware that she enjoyed the sensation of his voice, yet was completely freaked out by it at the same time.

"Only that you needn't be alone anymore; that part of your life is over Mara," the voice said. *"I've found you again."*

CHAPTER 2

Mara wrestled with the café's temperamental lock. She shivered as rain soaked through to skin, her supposedly waterproof coat useless against the current deluge. A disturbed night's sleep, filled with fitful, vivid dreams still hovered at the edges of her thoughts.

At last the key turned.

Inside, she warmed through quickly, her coat steaming next to the radiator as the oven flared to life. Instinctive routine took over; tension filled muscles relaxed as she measured, sifted, mixed.

Time was on her side this morning. The last of the cakes were in the oven, presenting an opportunity for some non-kitchen work. Taking a seat in the Victorian styled dining room, she began the next task; folding napkins around cutlery. Her eyes flicked around the cafe's interior as she worked, checking for other jobs.

The atmosphere of old-world luxury was something Mara always enjoyed. Dark, wood panelled walls, rich soft furnishings and shining brass transported her to another era. At least, it usually did. Today her mind had other ideas and all of them were focused on the voice in her head.

The condiments were full, the tablecloths spotless, the menus in place and the blue and white china shone invitingly on the fitted oak dresser. There was nothing left to do, and she still couldn't decide whether the voice was friend or foe. If it was the Lifelights, fine, but that last comment… worried her.

Mara glanced at the clock above the till. It was almost time to change the window sign to 'open' and Jennie still hadn't arrived. That in itself wasn't unusual, but today it made her nervous.

As if on cue the door swung inwards, but no leggy blonde stepped through the opening. A tall, lean figure appeared, wrapped in a rain soaked mac. The copy of The Times he carried looked equally soggy.

Mara's vision blurred as her eyes began to burn. Grabbing one of the napkins, still piled on the table, she ducked her head and dabbed at the tears spilling down her cheeks. *Oh no, not again.*

"Please excuse me; I'll be with you in a moment," she said. Pushing back her chair, she turned awkwardly towards the kitchen.

"Is there anything I can do to help?"

The man's voice was accented, American? It was also horribly familiar. Mara cringed, her eyes closing in automatic defence. *No... Not possible.*

Hands touched her shoulders, and a rush of heat flowed down her arms. It pooled in the palms of her hands, burning for a moment, before transforming into prickling sensation.

"Do you still not know me, Mara? Open your eyes. See me."

Stunned, Mara allowed herself to be turned. Her thoughts were chaotic. How could she fight something like this? It felt alien, yet right, scary, yet somehow comforting. His voice was more than words and inflection. Need and determination swept in behind it, strong emotions that flooded her mind, confusing her. The voice hadn't been the Lifelights then. *So who is this?*

At first his face was nothing more than irregular patches of light and shadow, shifting in and out of focus. Except for his eyes; they were blue-grey and... Recognition sparked, forcing its way out of her subconscious.

Her vision cleared, and she understood why Jennie had reacted as she had.

His warm skin tone mocked the English climate, stretched across sharply angled cheekbones, nose and jaw. His hair too seemed out of place, almost decadent. He wore it longer than most, the ends brushing against the shoulders of his coat, its chocolate brown strands dishevelled; raindrops clung to them.

She did know him... from somewhere. They'd met before, but she couldn't remember the details. *His name is...?*

"Sebastian," the voice whispered.

Sebastian? Yes, that was it. Silent laughter reached out, a shiver of movement that wrapped itself around her. She found the directness of his gaze disturbing. Maybe it was the subdued light, but for a moment she could have sworn that something sparked, deep within them. Silver? It swirled around dilated pupils before sinking from sight.

The lights in the café dimmed, flaring again as Mara pulled away. *Things like this don't happen. Not when I'm here, anyway.*

"Are you sure about that?" The voice asked. Mara nodded, barely registering that the voice seemed to be growing more adept at answering her thoughts. Unbidden, visions of the Lifelights rose up. That worried her, she clamped down on them, trying to blank her mind, to think of something else. No one could know about them, they were her secret. She knew that the Lifelights should be impossible. They shouldn't

exist, just like the voice in her head; but two things like that, happening to the same person? Not a chance. She was dreaming, or sick; maybe both.

Laughter echoed inside her head, its owner not bothering to hide his amusement.

Anger flared. *He thinks this is funny?* Mara opened her mouth to retort but stopped when the café door opened again and Jennie appeared, struggling with the usual tray of bread.

The man moved, taking hold of the door. Opening it wide, he waited until Jennie was clear. It gave Mara the release she needed. Stepping forward, she grabbed the opportunity with both hands.

"Jennie! Look at you, you're soaked. Here, give that to me."

The look of surprise that crossed her friend's face was almost comical, but Mara didn't care. Hastily, she snatched away the tray and headed for the kitchen. She placed it on the work surface, letting her hands flatten against the cool, practical steel. Bending her head, she breathed out a sigh of relief.

Shrill beeping shattered the silence and Mara jumped. The cakes were done. Taking them from the oven, she stared at them blankly for a moment. *What is it I need to do next?* Oh yes, the fillings.

The voices in the other room were a distraction. Jennie was clearly audible, chatting away, a deeper voice answering her.

Shaking off the urge to eavesdrop, Mara continued with the morning routine. First, she moved over to the coffee percolator, placing fresh grounds into the filter and checking the water level, before flicking the switch to 'on'. As her fingers brushed against the glass jug, it felt surprisingly warm. She frowned, hoping that it wasn't a wiring fault. She'd need to keep an eye on that.

Deciding on butter cream for the cakes, she reached for the ingredients, and then set about combining them... carefully. Small clouds of powdered sugar escaped from the bowl, flavouring the air.

Jennie came through the kitchen door and crossed to the sink. After washing her hands, she began to prepare sandwiches. Mara watched her out the corner of her eye.

Normally the two of them worked in easy, companionable silence, but today Mara's nerves were jangling.

"Anything you want me to do?" she asked.

Jennie didn't turn round, but Mara could see her smiling as she reached for another baguette. "Well, when you're ready, you can go and take Mr. Oran's order."

"Mr. Oran?" Mara didn't like the squeak of unease in her voice and hoped that it had gone undetected.

Jennie turned to look at her. "Yes, Mr. Oran. You know, our new customer, the one you let in a few minutes ago? He's very friendly, not at all stand-offish. I did wonder, after yesterday… but I was wrong. He's an American, did you know? Over here on business." Jennie paused for breath, staring at her hard, before asking "Is something wrong Mara?"

"No, nothing's wrong, I just thought you'd taken his order already. I heard you talking." Mara squirmed, unused to Jennie looking at her so intently.

"We were just having a bit of a chat. Mr. Oran wasn't ready for me to take his order. He suggested that I get on with my jobs and send you out in a few minutes."

"Why would he do that?" Mara regretted the words as soon as they left her mouth, watching with dismay as Jennie's eyebrows rose in tandem.

"Why wouldn't he?"

That, Mara realised, was a good question and one that she had no answer to.

With an apologetic grin, she shrugged "Sorry, he just makes me nervous. Take no notice."

Much to her relief, Jennie smiled back. "No need to apologise. Have to ask though, are you sure it's nerves you're feeling and not just your insides melting into a puddle? You've got to have noticed how yummy he is, or were you too chicken to check out his assets?" She waved the baguette she was holding, her eyes alight with mischief.

Mara looked pointedly at the baguette, "If his asset's that size, I think even you'd be chicken."

Jennie's mouth dropped open, her eyes widening with surprise. "Ooh, Mara Austin, that's *so* not like you. Go wash your mouth out with soap!"

Heat rushed into Mara's cheeks. Hurriedly she turned her back, ignoring the laughter behind her.

Once the butter cream was finished, she realised that the cakes were still too warm to assemble. Damn. She hesitated, though she knew there was only one option now.

It was time to find out what Mr. Oran wanted.

He was reading his newspaper as she entered the seating area. As she drew nearer, he lowered it, folded it into a neat oblong and slid it onto the table. His face was solemn as he watched her approach.

Standing a little further from him than she usually did when taking an order; Mara looked down at the order pad, gripping the pencil tightly. If she wanted to get through this, it was time to play ostrich.

There's nothing to be anxious about. He's just a customer.

She steadied her nerves by concentrating on breathing calmly and keeping any hint of a tremor from her voice.

"Are you ready to order now Mr. Oran?" Not too bad, but her voice was quieter than normal, with a slight husk to it. She'd have to work on that.

Her question was greeted with a sigh. "Aren't you even going to look at me, Mara?"

How does he know my name again? The saliva in her mouth seemed to have evaporated, making swallowing difficult. "Do you want a few more minutes to decide Mr. Oran?" *Stay professional.*

"No. I do want you to look at me though."

The order pad became the most fascinating thing that Mara had ever seen. She wondered who'd come up with the idea of spiral bound note pads; it really was a clever idea. Then she stilled, her gaze shifting as a hand came into her line of vision. It brushed against hers before stroking along the blue plaster wrapped around her index finger. Heat flooded the area, followed briefly by the same prickling sensation she'd felt earlier. Her pencil wobbled and fell to the floor. She watched, enthralled, as the plaster was peeled back to reveal...nothing.

"Does that feel better?" The voice enquired, its comforting tone sweeping through her mind.

Slowly, Mara looked up into the blue-grey eyes staring at her. Time crawled by as she found herself considering multiple possibilities, each one more bizarre than the one before. For several moments her mind was in chaos.

Taking a small step back, she forced herself to focus on the order pad again. "Are you ready to order now Mr. Oran?" She whispered.

A chuckle sounded, and the hand that held hers dropped away. Every muscle in her body was tensed, ready for flight, but she stayed in place. *This must be what a deer feels like, when it's caught in the headlights of an on-coming car.*

"Yes Mara, I suppose I am. I'd like tea please, and some toast with marmalade."

Bending to retrieve her pencil, Mara scribbled down the order. *That's it, act normal. 'Keep calm and carry on'.* As quickly as she dared, she turned on her heel, her stomach roiling with nerves.

"Good grief, are you okay?" Jennie was instantly concerned, as Mara leant against the kitchen worktop. She was shaking again. "What's the matter? You're white as a sheet. Are you feeling sick?"

Looking down at her right hand, Mara suppressed the bubble of hysterical laughter that threatened to escape. No, she wasn't sick, and now she literally didn't have a scratch on her. Not that she could tell Jennie that.

She needed an escape plan.

After a brief tussle with her conscience, Mara raised a hand, deliberately rubbing it across her forehead in a soothing motion. It wasn't all an act; her head was throbbing. "Actually, Jennie, I do feel a bit sick," she whispered.

"Oh, Mara, what are you saying?"

Ignoring the voice in her head, which she'd decided for her sanity's sake couldn't be real anyway, Mara allowed her eyes to plead with Jennie. She didn't want to face this now. She needed the Lifelights.

"You do look pale." Jennie said, "Perhaps you should go home."

Mara nodded, relieved, "I think you're right. Will you be able to manage on your own?"

"I'll be fine." Jennie said, "I managed, sort of, before you came to work for me. So don't you go worrying about *that*."

"Well, if you're sure. I really don't feel right."

Jennie nodded in understanding. “Are you okay getting home?”

“Yes, there’s a bus shortly. I’ll ring you if I’m no better by tonight, otherwise I’ll see you tomorrow. Thanks, Jennie. Oh and here’s Mr. Oran’s order. I really am sorry for leaving like this.”

Taking the order pad from her, Jennie wrapped a comforting arm around Mara’s shoulders as she began walking with her towards the café door. “Like I said, don’t worry about it. Just concentrate on getting yourself better.”

They had almost made it to the door when Mr. Oran’s voice halted them. “Is something the matter ladies?”

Mara instinctively froze, but Jennie turned to him with a friendly smile. “Nothing we can’t handle. Thanks for asking though. Mara’s feeling ill, so is going home. I hope you won’t mind waiting a few more minutes for your breakfast order?”

Reaching for her coat, Mara refused to look at their one and only customer as she shrugged herself into it. It was a shock to hear Mr. Oran’s chair being pushed back and find him standing only inches from her. His height and proximity were intimidating.

His voice, when it came, sounded concerned, “No, of course not,” he assured Jennie before turning towards Mara. “Do you need a lift anywhere? I don’t need to be at the office for another hour or so; I could drop you home if you’d like?”

Mara continued to avoid his eyes, shaking her head. Her body stiffened. His suggestion was absurd. *Do I look that stupid?* Number one golden rule of women’s safety - stay away from strangers’ cars.

Unfortunately, the fact that she could hear Mr. Oran’s amusement, whispering across her mind, proved that in certain areas he knew her intimately. It was a sobering thought.

Luckily, Jennie also knew the number one golden rule of women's safety. For the first time, suspicion edged her expression as she stared at their newest customer.

Mr. Oran appeared not to notice. His reply was as deep and smooth as ever. "No problem ladies, but if you ever do need my help Mara, here's my business card," he paused, "please, feel free to ring the number on it at any time. As you've probably gathered, I don't usually take notice of social boundaries. I find them too restrictive. I'm aware that my offer of a lift might seem strange to you, but it was meant as a goodwill gesture only."

Jennie's jaw visibly dropped at that. Apparently, Mr. Oran hadn't been as oblivious as he'd seemed. He couldn't have played the situation better if he'd tried.

Mara blew out a breath, impressed, as she realised that her friend had just switched allegiance. She felt something being pressed into her hand and looked down to see a thick, creamy white business card resting in her palm.

A glance at Jennie confirmed that she was still focused on Mr. Oran; enraptured at finding someone who shared her views on society's rules. Feeling strangely upset at being left out of the conversation, Mara slid the card into her pocket and left them to it.

Time to make good on that escape plan.

* * * *

It wasn't until much later, as Mara relaxed on her bed with the Lifelights crowding round her like concerned relatives, that she looked at the business card.

A swirling silver and black logo emblazoned the front of it, together with the words 'ORAN INDUSTRIES'. It went on to give Mr. Oran's name as Sebastian Oran, Chief Executive and stated that the company was the market leader in alternative energy research. The company's address, telephone number, fax details and website address were listed on the back.

Well, that was some of her questions answered, she supposed. Still, it didn't explain how she could hear him talking to her, in her head.

That was something she would dearly love to know the reason for. Failing that though, she was going to do exactly as Sebastian Oran had suggested and do a little checking on him.

"You could always ask me directly for the answers."

She scowled, as the ever patient voice invaded her thoughts. "Go away." She snapped.

His only response was deep laughter that teased her mind, making her want to smile in return. Not that she would. Whatever else Mara's life had made her, it had made her strong. Losing her parents at the age of three had started that process; losing her grandparents four years ago had finished the job. As long as she had the Lifelights though, nothing and no one was going to push her around.

"I heard you, you know. Our meeting was not an accident. I knew about you long before we met in person. Remember me, Mara."

"I think I asked you to go away." Mara said.

"How can I go away when I'm not actually with you?"

"Okay, let me rephrase that. Shut up. Do you understand me now?" Her hand thumped the quilt top and the Lifelights fluttered away in alarm.

There was no answer. It seemed that Mr. Oran had indeed understood and was doing as she asked. Gradually the Lifelights settled around her again and Mara could concentrate on the task she'd set herself.

It was time to do some research on her unexpected, unwelcome, telepathic 'friend'.

CHAPTER 3

"Good morning, Oran Industries."

It was well after lunch. Mara hadn't used the telephone number on the business card. She'd done as much online research into Oran Industries as she could before ringing the head office number given on their website. She glanced at her bedside clock in surprise when the phone was answered. She'd forgotten about the time difference.

"Good morning, I wonder if you could help me. My name is Mara Austin and…"

She didn't get any further, as the professional sounding woman on the other end of the line interrupted her. "Ah yes, Miss Austin, I was told to expect your call. If you would just hold for a moment, I'll put you through to Mr. Oran's office."

Mara hadn't expected *that*. Her heart started to race. There was a second's pause, then another voice, equally professional but more mature. "Good afternoon, Miss Austin. This is Alexa Munroe, Mr. Oran's Personal Assistant. How may I help you?" Here was someone who had no problem with the time difference.

That voice though… temporarily, Mara's own deserted her. *Why does Alexa Munroe sound familiar?*

Flustered, scrambling to re-direct her thoughts, Mara jumped in to speech, "Actually, I was after any information you can give me regarding Mr. Oran."

Silence reigned, the words *stupid, stupid, stupid* rushing through Mara's mind. Had she really expected the man's P.A. to hand over personal information to *her?*

Alexa Munroe's reply, after that brief hesitation, was smoothly delivered, "Of course, Miss Austin. As you are aware, Mr. Oran is currently in England, but he's asked that I give you my every assistance. If you'd give me your e-mail address, I can forward the information you need immediately."

This wasn't what Mara had expected, but she supposed that she should be grateful "Oh, well, that would be wonderful Ms. Munroe." She gave Alexa her e-mail details, and then thanked her for her help, before disconnecting the call. For several moments, she simply sat there, staring at her phone. *What, exactly, was that all about?*

Something tugged at her mind, testing boundaries that she'd been previously unaware of. Alexa's voice, just like Sebastian Oran, had blindsided her. It felt like… *déjà vu.*

True to Alexa Munroe's word, the information Mara wanted on Sebastian Oran hit her inbox minutes later. She was shocked to discover that it contained an in-depth biography, with several personal documents attached, giving her details of his date of birth, education and employment, residence particulars and marital status.

In a short space of time, sitting with her laptop balanced on the bed in front of her, Mara knew more about Sebastian Oran than she did about anyone else, barring herself. He was 34 years old, had been born in Italy, to an Italian Mother and American Father, and had his permanent base in the United States, both home and business. Oran Industries was his career baby, built from nothing into a global enterprise. From his education records, Mara also knew that he was highly intelligent and from the articles she had independently sourced, it appeared that he was widely respected, both by the business community and the charities he supported. He was also single, making him a magnet for the gossip columns, though from what Mara could tell, he fiercely defended his right to privacy.

And this was the same man who'd started eating at The Tea Cosy? It didn't make sense. Surely the café wasn't somewhere he'd normally spend time?

"Why are you so reluctant to see what is obvious, Mara? It's quite simple. I'm here because of you. You are the sole reason that I came into The Tea Cosy."

Mara stiffened, and then shivered. She wondered if she was ever really alone now.

A strange sensation buzzed through her. It took a moment for her to realise what it was, and that it wasn't all hers. Confusion, laced with impatience.

"You know me; have known me for a long time. I have waited years for this connection to re-form, so that I can speak to you like this. In time you'll be able to do the same, be able to control the link, but you can never break it. The years I've waited for you have not been easy, Mara."

Mara dropped her head into her hands as the words swirled through her mind. Oh God, what had she got herself into? This must be a mistake. Except for the Lifelights, her life was as unremarkable and unexciting as breakfast cereal. What could a man like Sebastian Oran possibly want with her?

"Why do we have this connection though?" She whispered, "Why me? Why now?"

Her question fell into silence, the hush of expectation stretching out across several seconds; her heart beats over-loud. Then Sebastian's voice returned, *"You have such a narrow view of the world, Mara. Your memories are incomplete, your current perception of reality flawed, but this will change. You are maturing, your body beginning to realise its true potential. Soon, your mind will follow its example. There is no need to be frightened."*

"But I *am* frightened." The admission slipped out of her as she flopped back against the pillows and stared at the Lifelights, now clustered around her and the laptop. Their glow was subtle in daylight, but still a comfort to her.

"No you're not, Mara. This has been a shock to you, yes, but don't confuse that with fear. You will remember. You need time, that's all."

She allowed herself a small smile. *That's the understatement of the decade.* She'd be old and grey before she accepted the sound of his voice in her head.

Laughter permeated every corner of her mind, and she briefly wondered if Sebastian Oran was ever miserable. He always seemed to be laughing. *"Old and grey, Mara? I haven't seen you like that for a long time. And even if I wanted to, I cannot wait 'till then. Our gifts bind us together. The attraction we feel is not an option."*

Mara tensed. *Attraction?* Nope, she wasn't touching that word or the 'old and grey' comment. Instead, she latched onto the other shocking suggestion, "Gifts?"

Again, he laughed, *"Forgive me; you're not ready to hear that. Just accept that you're different, and that I'm here. The rest will come."*

Sound rumbled its way through tensed vocal cords, emerging as a low growl. "Easy for you to say, you're not the one with an annoying, *strange*, man running around your head."

"True, but I do have an extremely stubborn woman in mine."

Mara couldn't stop the smile that curved her mouth, as his irritation filtered through to her. "And whose fault is that, Mr. Oran?"

"Not mine, I assure you. It was your mind, crying out to me, that started this. And please, my name is Sebastian. Call me by it."

Mara scowled at that, aware that his irritation had shifted into arrogance. She glared at the image on the screen in front of her. It showed a smiling 'Mr. Oran', at some charity event or other. She shut the laptop with a snap. It was bad enough having him in her head, talking nonsense, without having to look at him.

"Sebastian." He whispered, before the connection faded.

* * * *

She was in a bad mood for the rest of the day. The Lifelights, as usual, responded to her mental state, crowding round her as she struggled with her thoughts. They touched her constantly, tingles sweeping across her skin with each contact. Their attention made her feel cherished, but her stress levels continued to rise.

The atmosphere in the cottage felt oppressive, as if charged with the same muscle tightening emotions that rolled through Mara. It was an idea that gathered credence as the day progressed. She began to receive tiny electric shocks, like static discharge, as she moved around her home. The crackle and mild pain of each pulse did nothing to improve her mood, and in the end she avoided anything metallic.

In the evening Jennie phoned to check on her. Even the telephone spat out electricity. Glaring at her throbbing fingers, Mara still admitted that she was feeling better and reassured her friend that she'd be at work the following day.

Several hours later, back in bed and trying to get to sleep, Mara confronted the truth. The Lifelights had always been her security blanket. Yes, they were strange, inexplicable even, but she accepted their presence as natural, just as her grandparents had. It had never occurred to her to question what they were or why they were in the cottage.

Because of the Lifelights, she had an open mind when it came to supernatural abilities. The thought of telepathy didn't faze her. Sebastian Oran, on the other hand… did.

Why is he so focused on me? Does he know about the Lifelights?

She hoped not. The Lifelights were special; secret.

So now what? Sebastian wasn't going to give up, he'd said as much. Mara frowned; glad that she was going back to work tomorrow. At least the café was neutral ground.

Debating her options, Mara wondered if she should do as Sebastian suggested and try to get to know him better. She had a sneaking suspicion that it was the only way she'd get to the truth of what was happening to her.

"Happening, to us."

Mara plumped up her pillow. "Go away Sebastian. I'm tired."

"I can never really leave you, Mara. I've told you this already. Sleep well though, and dream of me. I'll see you in the morning."

Oh, wonderful.

Mara's grouchy reply, "That's what I was afraid you'd say," was met with a quiet chuckle, as her eyelids grew heavy. Her dreams were rife with Lifelights, electric shocks and blue-grey eyes.

CHAPTER 4

Stones skittered underfoot as she dashed down the cottage's driveway.

This was ridiculous. She'd lived with supernatural 'lights' since the age of three and was currently dealing with the attentions of an American telepath. So why couldn't she grasp something as basic as setting her alarm clock?

On the plus side, she couldn't hear the bus yet. Hopefully it was running late this morning.

As she neared, the reason for the lack of polluting noise became clear.

Relief poured through her. Thank goodness for Mr. Thompson, the world's best bus driver.

The bus was parked opposite her driveway, the engine switched off.

Finding an extra burst of speed for the last few yards, Mara arrived at its open doors, breathless and flushed.

She came to a shocked halt; *of all the devious...*

Mr. Thompson interrupted her train of thought, smiling down at her from behind the steering wheel. "Good morning, pretty girl."

Every morning, his greeting was the same.

What wasn't the same as other mornings was the tall, tailored figure leaning casually against the ticket machine, looking as if he had every right to be there.

Sebastian Oran.

She stared in consternation from one man to the other.

Her brain hadn't managed to form a coherent sentence, let alone got one as far as her mouth.

Mr. Thompson began speaking again, "Mr. Oran was just explaining about your new travel arrangements, young lady. Have to say, I'm going to miss seeing you on here, but can't say that I blame you either. It's going to be a whole lot comfier travelling in that beauty."

Mr. Thompson's eyes crinkled, his mouth turning up into the familiar smile that Mara loved. He nodded his head towards the front of the bus.

After glaring at Sebastian, who pretended not to notice, smiling innocently, she turned her head to look through the bus' windscreen.

Parked a little way ahead, hugging both verge and tarmac with its fluid, low-slung design, a lustrous black car screamed for attention. The early morning light highlighted every precise, sculpted curve. How had she missed that?

Despite herself, Mara blinked.

"But…" her traitor of a brain still wasn't giving her anything sensible to say.

Sebastian took immediate advantage. Turning towards Mr. Thompson, he shook his hand, "It was a pleasure to meet you Mr. Thompson. And please, don't worry; I'll take good care of your 'pretty girl'."

He raised his hand to wave to the other passengers. Amazingly, several waved back. They seemed unconcerned by the delay to their journey.

Mara struggled to form a protest, but a moment later she was pushed backwards. Firm hands steadied her, as she stumbled on the uneven grass verge. Sebastian stepped to one side, taking her hand in his.

She wasn't brave enough to cause a scene.

Raising her hand in a reflexive wave, she watched as the bus pulled away. It disappeared around the next bend in the road, and the reality of her situation hit home. It was just the two of them now, standing beside a deserted country road.

The thought that she should be screaming at this point or at the very least, running, crossed her mind. She did neither.

Considering the surreal quality of the last two days, maybe that wasn't so surprising.

How had Sebastian put it? 'You needn't be alone anymore, I've found you again.'

The words didn't sound like a threat after all. They were merely a statement of fact. Sebastian Oran believed that he had every right to be here.

She turned, tilting her head back so that she could look directly into his face. "Okay, you win. What's next?"

His arrogant satisfaction filled her mind as he released her hand, curling his arm around her shoulders instead. A jolt rippled through Mara's muscles as he pulled her against his side, the bunched fibres flexing beneath his touch.

Trepidation, excitement and confusion fought for supremacy inside her.

She wasn't experienced with men, not at all, but she wasn't stupid either.

Through Jennie, she'd experienced relationships vicariously, acting as a sympathetic agony sponge on more than one occasion. Though they'd been one sided, she'd learnt enough through their girlie chats to recognise the truth of what Sebastian had said the evening before.

The attraction between them was real, but she hadn't a clue what to do with it.

For a moment, she allowed herself to consider what it would be like to give in. How would it feel to explore what was between them? The possibilities... her breath sped up. *Wait, what am I thinking*?

"Interesting thoughts."

Mara glanced at Sebastian; which was a mistake.

He has mesmerising eyes. Flashes of silver light raced, vortex like, around intense black pupils, easily pulling her deeper, into the man himself.

She leaned towards him, fascinated and curious.

Then he blinked, and she stilled.

"You begin to see, I think. You are 'my' Mara."

As with the Lifelights, it was the emotions that Sebastian triggered, together with a confusing mass of awareness, which had the strongest effect.

Mara allowed their impact to flow through her.

She was aware of her blood, hot and alive, coursing through her veins. It was as if champagne flowed alongside corpuscle and plasma, fizzing and bubbling its way around her body. It rushed from organ to organ, raising her temperature further, expanding her emotions and senses, until all reason had been pushed aside, leaving her light-headed.

The epiphany hit her, head-on. Whoever Sebastian Oran was, he couldn't, wouldn't be ignored. He was important to her. It was time she accepted that.

A part of her had died with her parents; she'd always known that. A piece of her soul had gone AWOL.

For the first time in nineteen years, Mara wondered if she'd found it again. Was she looking at it now, in the shape of a man who refused to take 'no' for an answer?

Need. Hope. It had been a long time since she'd felt either of those.

She knew that she would never have survived without the love she'd received from her grandparents and the Lifelights, but that was all she'd done.

The thought of finally starting to 'live' was tempting.

Sebastian capitalised on her stillness.

She could feel him in her mind, almost intrusive, examining the thoughts holding her captive.

He stepped closer, tightening his arm around her shoulders, before bending his head slowly towards hers. For a moment she thought that he was going to kiss her, but instead he pressed his mouth close to her ear and breathed out slowly.

Delicious warmth cascaded across the sensitive nerves of her neck and down her spine. Then he spoke, "To answer your question Mara, next I drive you to work. Then we talk, this morning, this evening, for as long as we need to and by whatever means we can. You have questions. I understand that. Your concerns need to be addressed. However, know this, we have a bond; one that will only grow stronger. The outcome of our meeting, our future relationship, is already determined."

Mara shivered.

She found his voice disturbing. It tugged at something in her mind, the pitch and cadence strangely familiar. It comforted her, warmed her.

He pulled away, waiting until she gave him a nod of understanding. His fingers brushed along her shoulder and down the line of her spine. His hand pressed against her back, steering her towards the side of the car.

It was only as her hand touched the cold metal of the door, which he held open for her, that she stopped.

Her inbuilt fear of getting into strange cars, drilled into her over the years, was strong. It warred with an equally strong urge to do what Sebastian wanted. In that moment of hesitation, her brain unexpectedly threw out a question.

"What sort of car is this? I don't think I've seen one like it before."

His hand stroked along the top of the door, his expression somewhat smug. He covered her fingers with his. "Do you know; I'm not quite sure… yet. Why don't we find out? Of course, as with most things, the make is insignificant. It's the hidden potential that's exciting."

His gaze linked with hers, "Don't you agree?"

With a shrug, she decided that it really didn't matter.

She swallowed her remaining nerves and allowed herself to be guided into the passenger seat.

Sebastian waited patiently while she was settled, then closed the door with a soft thud.

Mara found herself in another world.

She'd never been in a car as luxurious as this. The seat beneath her hugged her body, moulding her small frame. She liked it, and that surprised her. Personal fears notwithstanding, she'd always believed that she was the wrong sex to appreciate cars.

This was something different though and she began to see what Sebastian had meant.

The car *felt* alive, humming with potential, even without the engine running.

Excited anticipation filled her. *Another first*, she thought.

Seating himself next to her, Sebastian threw out a smile, the silver in his eyes sparkling. "Are you ready for this?"

Her heart picked up its pace. "I think so. This is going to be something special isn't it?"

He didn't answer immediately. Instead, he turned towards the dashboard.

With a touch of his hand, the car's engine came alive.

"Oh yes Mara, with you on board, it's going to be spectacular. Didn't you know? Cars are like men; they can't help showing off in front of the ladies."

That was all the warning she got.

The power of acceleration forced Mara deep into her seat.

The countryside flashed past, as tarmac disappeared beneath them with ever increasing speed. Tiny flashes of light decorated the dashboard, Sebastian's movements confident and precise as he steered them round each bend. Mara's heartbeat quickened with every twist and turn.

She relished the experience, astonished that she could, as exhilaration eclipsed fear. This was a car like no other. This was a car she could come to covet.

Even though he took the longest possible route between Mara's home and The Tea Cosy, they still completed the journey in record time, pulling up in front of the café a good ten minutes before she usually arrived.

She exhaled, letting out her breath with a soft 'whoosh'.

Sebastian was clearly pleased with himself, as she turned towards him. "So, come on, spill the beans. What kind of car is this really?" She asked.

He grinned, "It's an Oran Industries prototype."

She rolled her eyes, "Oh come on Sebastian. Even I know that companies keep their prototypes securely under wraps. If this car really was a prototype, it'd be locked up, being tested to destruction in some secret lab, not racing round the English countryside."

She held up her hand when Sebastian looked as if he was going to argue, before continuing, "And don't tell me it's 'okay', because you're the boss. Regardless, I won't believe you."

"But it's the truth!" Sebastian protested, "I'm not just the Chief Executive at Oran Industries, I also have a hand in the designing and testing of some of our products."

"Uh huh, and I'm a secret billionaire!"

Mara began to get cross, wondering why he'd bother lying to her about this.

"But I'm not lying. Just because you won't believe me, doesn't mean I'm not telling you the truth, my Mara."

His eyes were amused.

Mara scowled in response. "Stop calling me 'your' Mara and *stop* with the mind talking. Keep out of my head Mr. Oran and keep your thoughts to yourself."

"Oh Mara, don't start that again, please. I thought you'd got over being bothered by this?"

"I had, sort of, but if you aren't going to talk sense then don't bother, with either with your mouth or your mind!"

A smile curled at the corners of his mouth, "Okay Mara, you win this time. If I show you what's under the hood, will you at least try to keep an open mind?"

She remained suspicious, but then decided it would be churlish to refuse, grabbing her things and opening her door.

She swung her legs round onto the pavement and stood up.

He'd extended his hand, but she ignored his offer of assistance.

Shrugging, he turned to open and secure the bonnet, before casually walking away, over to a nearby lamppost, where he leant, arms folded and eyes watchful.

She was irritated to find that she was disappointed, wanting him nearer.

Mara turned her attention to the car.

Before her was something she recognised. She'd covered the pros and cons of electric motor v combustion engine in Science at School. Her frown deepened as she looked across at Sebastian. "But… I don't understand?"

"I said this car is a prototype, Mara. I didn't say that what's under the hood is the prototype. I also didn't mention that this particular car will never be on general release. It will be made in limited numbers, personalised to specific customers."

Mara was uncertain of the significance of that last piece of information.

She decided to concentrate on the first part of what Sebastian had said. "But your company deals with alternative energy, the fact that this car runs on electricity is testament to that. This motor doesn't look any different to the others I've seen though, so if it's not that, then it must be a new way of..."

Her eyes widened, as something in her brain clicked into place.

She quickly made a circuit of the car, her eyes running over its smoothly sculpted lines. "Where's the re-charge point for the battery?"

He didn't reply. Instead, he stretched out a hand and studied it carefully, before speaking. "Are you going to apologise, Mara?"

He deserved one. She'd all but called him a liar.

With a concerted effort, Mara tried to make her apology count. She thought rather than spoke her reply, attempting to push the words out from her mind.

"I suppose I do owe you an apology, Sebastian."

He stilled, his eyes rising to stare at her in disbelief, before he grinned, a warmth spreading through his blue-grey eyes as he bounded across the space between them.

He picked her up before she had a chance to avoid him, swinging her round. When he set her down again, she found herself cradled against him. She watched with fascination as he raised one hand and gently stroked down the side of her face.

Everywhere his fingers touched, her skin tingled in response.

His expression held pride, as words flooded her mind. *"Apology accepted, my clever girl. I was wondering when you'd speak to me like this. I knew you could do it if you tried."*

His stare was intense.

She drew in a deep breath, making her decision. She was twenty two... old enough to handle this. Hopefully.

She mentally followed the movements of his hand, rubbing its way, in soothing sweeps, across her back. Her voice was hesitant, when she finally forced herself to speak.

"So, it's not the engine that's prototype. It's the fuel."

Mara closed her eyes in disgust. What a wimp. Why did she say that?

Sebastian gave a grudging nod. "*Yes.* It's the fuel that's prototype. And as the fuel isn't part of the car, I can use it without fear of anyone discovering our secret."

His hand caressed.

He looked smug again. Wait, did he just pull her closer?

She considered letting go of her inhibitions, but it was another thing to do it.

His other hand had moved to her chin, tilting it upwards. She could easily see the silver light in his eyes. It made her feel strange, overheated.

She'd be brave another time. Just not right now.

After all, they were standing outside The Tea Cosy; not the best place to explore their attraction to each other.

Mara took a physical step back.

"How can a fuel source be separate to the car? It doesn't make sense; the motor needs something to power it."

"Indeed it does. Unfortunately, that's the information that's secret and 'prototype'. I couldn't possibly tell you how it works. Not unless I kidnapped you to keep you from telling or…." Sebastian stopped abruptly, his smile turning calculating and a little wicked.

Mara knew she shouldn't ask, "Or what?"

"Or you could always try prying my secrets from me through pillow talk. What do you think? I might be so overcome by you that I won't be able to help myself. Potentially, I could tell you everything you want to know."

This sudden, uncharacteristic suggestion from the ever controlled Sebastian Oran came as a shock. After a moment of stunned silence, Mara moved. Something was stirring inside her, daring her.

Her mind as blank as possible, she smiled up at him, deliberately sweet.

Her eyes gazed into his as she raised her left foot, before slamming it down onto the top of his.

The force behind it caused him to jump back, an expression of shock flashing out at her.

She grinned back, following the move with a quick, hard, shove to his chest. She wasn't sure if she'd caught him off-balance or simply by surprise, but it didn't matter.

He staggered.

She turned upon her heel, marching over to The Tea Cosy's door and rummaging for her key, just getting it into the lock as she heard the car being locked and felt Sebastian come up behind her.

He crowded her into the wood panelling, his hands landing on either side of her. *"That was uncalled for, 'my' Mara, you should apologise again."*

The café door swung inwards, and Mara gave a heartfelt laugh of relief as she stepped across the threshold. Spinning round, she felt the bravery enhancing 'something' rushing through her. She was enjoying herself.

With space between them once again, she turned to grin at him, unrepentant. "No, I won't be apologising. You were moving way too fast Sebastian. You deserved everything you got."

He watched her, his eyes assessing, brighter than ever in the café's dim light. Then he too grinned, his face taking on a mischievous expression. This was a side of him that Mara hadn't encountered before. It suited him.

"Okay, have it your own way. You have to admit though; it might have been fun. Think of all those corporate secrets you've missed out on. Ah well, perhaps you'd better get on with your work. I'll sit, and watch you bake. I haven't got to be anywhere for at least an hour. It will give me an idea of how things will be… when we're together."

"In your dreams," she thought, trying to glare, whilst ignoring the urge to laugh... and the inner glow, slowly spreading through her.

CHAPTER 5

By the time Jennie arrived, Sebastian was sitting at the table with the best view of the kitchen. He watched Mara as she worked, whilst sipping the strong black coffee he'd convinced her he needed.

Mara felt flushed; the heat of the kitchen only part of the equation. Every time she allowed her eyes to stray, Sebastian's blue-grey gaze met hers. The inner silver would spark as his mouth curved into a small, satisfied smile.

He was, she'd decided, lethal. He disturbed her to a point that she *should* run in the opposite direction.

Not that there was any real danger of that.

The man had taken up squatters rights inside her brain but, perversely, she was happier now than she had been for a long time. She wasn't sure whether that was because of the telepathy, the eye-candy or said eye-candy's sheer, bloody-minded persistence.

Her only real worry was the Lifelights.

Trying to decide what her options were gave Mara a headache. Her mind returned to the same arguments again and again. She pushed the thoughts away and concentrated on her work.

Jennie didn't comment on Sebastian's presence in the café before opening time. She did, however, give him a flirtatious wink as she sashayed past him and grinned at Mara as she came into the kitchen.

"Something looks yummy," she said, licking her lips and waggling her eyebrows

It was quite an achievement, like rubbing your tummy whilst patting your head. Not for the first time Mara wished for some of what her friend had. Viewing men as treats to be savoured was a skill she'd never mastered. Not even close.

"The chocolate cake?" She asked, pretending not to understand.

"No, silly, the beefcake," Jennie rolled her eyes and jabbed a thumb back towards Sebastian's table.

"If you say so," Mara said.

Jennie laughed, "Are you sure you're feeling better, darling? You seem to be having problems with your vision."

Mara ignored her and Jennie's grin widened. "So, moving swiftly on, whose mean machine is parked outside?"

"Whose do you think?" Mara nodded towards Sebastian.

He, in turn, raised his coffee cup in salute to them.

Jennie fluttered her eyelashes at him before whispering, loud enough for him to hear, "You could do worse you know. Not only is the man good looking, but with a car like that and his interest in you, he also seems to have good taste."

Mara blushed. She tried to make her reply casual, "You'd think so wouldn't you? I suspect he has enough bad habits to counteract the good points though. Either way, I haven't made my mind up about Mr. Oran yet."

"You are such a liar. Why don't you just admit it, you've already accepted my presence here. We're on to the next phase now."

Jennie moved into the dining room with a handful of mail, leaving Mara to get on with the washing up and practice her scowl. Did Jennie *have* to swing her hips like that when she passed Sebastian's table? If she kept it up, dislocation was a distinct possibility.

She took comfort in allowing her mind to answer him, *"And what is the next phase?"*

"The one where I dazzle you with my courtship, before seducing you into committing yourself to me... again," Sebastian replied.

The measuring jug Mara was cleaning slipped from her grasp and dropped into the washing up bowl with a thud. It created a plume of soapy water, which splashed over the side of the sink and down her top.

His amusement flowed across her mind. She heard him cough in an attempt to disguise his verbal laughter. It was a pitiful camouflage. Jennie, going through the morning's post, looked at him questioningly.

He pointed to the newspaper he was reading.

"There are some good jokes in this morning's edition," he explained, now laughing openly. Jennie shrugged, before going back to the bill she was reading. Mara couldn't help smiling.

"Now who's lying?"

"Getting the hang of this, aren't you, my Mara?" was his only reply.

There was the sound of a chair being scraped back; Mara looked towards the dining area. Jennie had risen from her seat and crossed to the electricity cupboard in the corner. Opening it, she glanced from the bill in her hand to the digits displayed on the meter. Her brow furrowed in concentration.

Sebastian had stilled. To a casual observer, it would probably have looked as if he was still reading his newspaper. Mara knew different though. As attuned to him as she was, she could see that his eyes were trained on Jennie.

Was his interest in her waning already?

"Green doesn't suit you, my darling. Jennie's feeling stressed. Haven't you noticed?"

After a minute of quiet study, he spoke.

"You look worried Jennie, anything the matter? Electricity Supplier trying to say you owe them more than you do?"

Jennie waved a hand absently towards his table, "No, actually, the reverse," she murmured before closing the cupboard again and writing something at the top of the bill. Once that was done, she looked up at Sebastian and smiled, "If I get any more of these types of bills, I may even have to use my secret weapon."

"What secret weapon?" Sebastian asked.

"Miss Maths Genius over there…" Jennie said, nodding towards Mara, "If anyone can sort out this mess, it's her."

Mara laughed, holding up her dripping hands, encased in a pair of yellow rubber gloves, "Yeah, right. If I really was a Maths genius, do you think I'd be wearing these cool fashion accessories voluntarily?"

She went back to the washing-up. It was only when she heard another chair being moved that she glanced up. Sebastian was standing by the ornate, antique brass till, paying Jennie for his drink

"Well ladies, much as I hate to leave you, the office calls. I have back-to-back meetings for most of the day. I hope I have your sympathy." His voice was low, forlorn almost, causing Jennie to make suitably compassionate noises. Mara found herself smirking as she listened, amazed at how easily Sebastian was insinuating himself into her friend's 'good-books'.

She didn't like the way it made her feel, knowing that he was leaving. Her stomach clenched, tension tightening her shoulders and neck. Not knowing what to say, she remained silent. She concentrated on the baking sheet she was washing, scouring it with renewed vigour.

She jumped when he appeared in the kitchen doorway.

He stayed there, waiting patiently, until she finally gave-in and acknowledged him.

The strange connection they shared rushed through her mind, causing her to shiver.

"I'll be back to pick you up this evening, Mara. Don't bother getting the bus. I'm going right past your home, so it makes sense for me to drop you off on the way."

Unsure what to say, Mara just stared at him. Then her eyes moved to Jennie, whose mouth had fallen open in surprise. Annoyed that he had put her in this situation, she tried to look surprised by his offer.

"Oh, well, that's very kind of you, Sebastian. If you're sure it won't be any trouble?"

Jennie's expression grew smug. Belatedly Mara realised that she'd called Sebastian by his first name. Something she shouldn't really know.

Shrugging, he grinned at the two of them before turning towards the door. "It's no trouble at all. I'll meet you outside after you've locked-up."

As the door shut behind him, Mara turned, bracing herself for the avalanche of questions she could sense on Jennie's lips. One wrong move and she'd be swept away.

Thankfully she was rescued by a group of their regular customers, in need of breakfast. What a shame they wouldn't have time to chat after all. She exited the kitchen, order pad in hand, before Jennie had a chance to draw breath.

Of course, she couldn't avoid her all day.

The offensive started without preamble. Jennie barely allowed Mara to take a sip of her break-time drink, before she began her interrogation.

"So, come on, what's been happening between you and Mr. 'Gorgeous' Oran? He's interested in you… that much is obvious. Has he asked you out yet?"

Jennie was certainly direct.

"Look, honestly, nothing's happened, and I'm *so* not getting into the 'is he interested' debate. No, he hasn't asked me out. He gave me a lift to work this morning and, as you heard, is giving me a lift home tonight. That's it."

"But how did he know where you live Mara? He hasn't been stalking you has he?"

Mara laughed at that and launched into the part of her story that was sheer fabrication, as far as she knew.

"No, he's renting a property in the village just up from me. He says he prefers it to staying in a hotel and he enjoys country living more than being in town. The villages are the perfect place for him to stay whilst he's here.

"As for the lift, it was sheer coincidence that he spotted me at the bus stop this morning. I was shocked when he pulled up and asked if I wanted a lift." Carefully, Mara took a sip of her drink. She concentrated on keeping her hand steady, as she placed the cup back on the table.

She hated lying.

"I thought it was very nice of him to offer." She said.

Jennie raised her eyebrows, leaning across the table towards her, "Oh yeah, very nice of him. You *do* realise he fancies you, don't you? Take it from an expert; he'd be on you like a flash if you gave him the chance."

Mara could feel her cheeks heating up.

"Don't be ridiculous. If anything, it's the atmosphere in here he enjoys. If you think about it, it made sense for him to give me a lift. He got to come in here before the rush, sit down and drink his coffee in peace."

"Hmm," Jennie sounded far from convinced. "Of course, that makes perfect sense. It doesn't explain why he was ogling you though."

Unable to stop herself, Mara groaned, glaring at Jennie with as much indignation as she could muster. "Mr. Oran was not ogling me!"

Jennie laughed.

"Oh, it's 'Mr. Oran' now is it? It was 'Sebastian' earlier on." She paused, her eyes sparkling with amusement as she watched Mara over the top of her coffee cup. "You really should just come out and admit it you know. You like him and he likes you. What's so scary about that? They don't come much better packaged and it's about time you started dating."

Mara threw up her hands in a gesture of defeat, before finishing her drink and standing up. "You're impossible, you know that? Sebastian is being a gentleman. He's giving me a lift to and from work. No big deal. Anyway, I thought you were interested in him? You were swinging those hips for England earlier on. It's a wonder you didn't take his eye out."

"Ooh, were you jealous, darling?" Jennie teased, grinning, "You know me, and I love to flirt. I'm practicing for when I meet Mr. Right. However, as it's you he's got his eye on, I'm more than happy to back off. You go for it girl."

Mara stared at her friend, "Go for it? Are you mad? Mr. Oran is only visiting England, Jennie. That makes whether I like him or not a moot point, because I'm definitely not interested in a brief 'fling'."

The last comment was designed to overcome any of the arguments Jennie was considering using. Unfortunately, it didn't work like that.

Jennie whistled at her tart tone of voice, "Uh huh, and you really have got it bad, no matter what you tell yourself."

Mara felt like crying with frustration. She was stopped by a whisper in her mind.

"Why do you do this to yourself? You must know that I'm not going anywhere. Not without you. Our future is already set. Even Jennie can see how right we are for each other. Just relax, and try to remember. As I said, we have entered the next phase of our relationship. Let it happen..."

If there had been anything in the café to kick, Mara would have. Instead, she continued through her working day on automatic.

She ignored the knowing looks that Jennie gave her. It proved more difficult to deny the excitement and anticipation that grew inside her as closing time approached.

True to his word Sebastian was waiting outside, leaning against the wall of the café. He appeared relaxed but remained statue still as he watched them lock up. Only his eyes moved, as they tracked Mara.

Jennie grinned as she said goodbye.

Sebastian's gaze was focused, his face set in determined lines, as he crossed over to Mara's side. He took hold of her arm and guided her towards the car, opening the passenger door with old world courtesy.

Jennie would love watching this. A quick glance at her friend's face as she drove past, waving, and Mara knew the questions would start again tomorrow.

All thoughts of Jennie disappeared though, when Sebastian slid into the seat beside her.

The effect he had on her was profound. Her breathing became slightly uneven and her heart rate shot up when he closed the door behind him. There was such a small space between them. In a strange way, the close confines of the car managed to feel intimate.

Neither of them spoke as the car was once again put through its paces.

Mara was too busy worrying about what to do/say when they got to the end of the journey and Sebastian seemed content to let her stew. It was only when they pulled onto the road that ran past the cottage that she found her voice.

"You can drop me off at the end of the driveway if you like; I don't want to be any bother."

Damn. Could her voice sound *more* breathless?

Sebastian didn't reply. He shot her what she now considered to be his signature, amused, look. A second later Mara heard his voice in her mind again.

"Oh, no you don't Mara. As I think I said this morning, we are now in the next phase. I am courting you my dear. If you remember, that's the bit that comes before the seducing part of my plan. So I couldn't possibly abandon you at the end of your driveway."

He turned his head to look at her briefly, his expression wicked, "I'll take you to your door and then you'll politely invite me in for a coffee. Isn't that how it's done?"

"I wouldn't know Mr. Oran." She tried to sound aloof. Not an easy thing to do, when her heart was beating at nineteen to the dozen.

The car turned into the driveway, crunching over the gravelled surface.

As they pulled to a stop outside the cottage, Mara felt panic begin to rise.

Sebastian touched his hand to the dashboard and the motor fell silent.

"You know, Mara, I find the rather severe way you say 'Mr. Oran' strangely alluring. Are you deliberately trying to entice me?"

Mara jumped as Sebastian's voice filled the car. The fact that he'd spoken aloud was no comfort at all. With each word, he leant forward, closer, until he was inches away from her.

His eyes never left hers.

She could feel the warmth of his breath against her lips.

There were so many unfamiliar emotions coiling through her; she was at a loss as to what to do next.

"Next you are going to invite me into your home for a coffee, remember?" Sebastian was clearly enjoying her confusion. It appeared that he had no qualms about using it to his advantage.

Mara, however, was not so far gone that the thought of the Lifelights had vanished. She opened her mouth to explain that it was impossible for him to come in, when she heard his voice again. It sounded deep, serious.

"Come now, my Mara, I am sure your beautiful Lifelights will love me on sight. Don't you want to introduce me to your family?"

The words were unexpected, shocking. She had no option but to reply to them through her newly acquired skill. Her vocal chords refused to work.

"How do you know about the Lifelights?"

Sebastian's expression became grave, his eyes guarded.

"My beautiful girl, how could I not know about them? They are a part of you, more than you could possibly realise. Their light defines you, right down to your soul."

If the depth of emotion in his words hadn't taken Mara's breath away, then the kiss that followed did. Sebastian closed the gap between them so fast, she was hardly aware that he had moved, until the maelstrom hit her.

This was no hesitant first kiss.

It was a demonstration of passion.

Sebastian's mouth was firm, using her surprise to give him the entry he needed to deepen the kiss. He dominated every movement, as his mind thrust into hers, releasing a mass of erotic images that stripped away all pretence of courtship. A host of confusing, jumbled thoughts slammed into Mara's unsuspecting mind. They flooded her consciousness, demanding acknowledgement. His need roared out, laying waste to flimsy mental defences.

After the initial seconds of shock Mara responded, her own need rising. Fierce exploration took over. Her hands moved of their own volition, eyelids drifting down. The reality of her surroundings faded, allowing her to focus on the feel of his lips, tongue and teeth. Resistance slipped away.

She had only been kissed once before… a long time ago, at a school party. It had been nothing more than an inexperienced, awkward, meeting of lips. So what was this? Memories encroached, unfamiliar pictures of other times, other kisses and more.

Mara didn't want it to stop. As the kiss went on she became aware of her senses expanding. Especially touch. The feel of Sebastian's hands moving over her, heated her skin. A shiver of energy flowed across every inch of her. It pooled in the curves of her body, the sweep of her neck, her shoulders, the hollow along her spine, the dip of her waist, the deep V where thigh met hip. Every nerve responded. They tingled into life with a charge of sensuality.

Where their lips met and hands touched, the heat built. It was as if an electric current passed between them, looping around in a closed circuit.

The wrench as Sebastian raised his head, breaking the kiss, had Mara's eyes flying open again and moaning in protest. His eyes shone back at her, the bright silver making them almost iridescent. Triumph blazed without apology.

"Invite me in."

The last barrier fell.

With a single nod Mara crossed the point of no return.

CHAPTER 6

Mara turned her key in the lock, every nerve in her body alert.

Sebastian stood silently beside her.

The only contact between them was the hand he rested against the small of her back, its warmth radiating through her blouse. A small shiver of apprehension ran down Mara's spine, and Sebastian responded immediately. His fingers splayed, the warmth from his hand spreading across her skin.

"Don't be nervous; this is how it's meant to be. You'll see."

Pushing the front door wide, Mara wasn't so sure. Her eyes scanned the hallway in front of them, automatically searching for the Lifelights.

"This is one of the scariest things I've ever done. I've never let anyone see the Lifelights before. Are you sure you want to do this?"

The hand at her back pressed harder, urging her forward.

"Oh yes. I've been waiting nineteen years for this. It's time."

The door shut behind them with a distinctive 'click'. Mara's eyes took a moment to adjust to the low light levels, and then she saw them.

They were hovering above the staircase, together, gathered into a ball of light.

What were they doing?

The air in the hallway was cold, thickened by tension. Though she'd never had the guts to try it, Mara wondered if this was how skydivers felt as they prepared to jump. Did they stare out across the sky before they stepped into nothingness? Did they allow the bite of fear to test their resolve?

Fear didn't come close to describing how she felt at this moment. Terror was closer.

Was she doing the right thing?

"Yes. Watch them. Reach out to them as you did to me. Try to remember."

As a single mass the Lifelights rose from their position on the stairs and moved across the hallway, until they hovered above the two of them. The shape they'd formed held firm, a three dimensional sphere. The outline of it was static, but groups of four Lifelights twirled from one position to another within the outer boundary.

"I think they like me."

Sebastian's whisper glided through Mara's mind as she struggled to take in what she was seeing. She felt him step away, moving his hand from her back as he did so, to thread his fingers through hers. Their linked hands became a bridge between them.

The Lifelights within the sphere moved faster. Suddenly it split into two, as cleanly as a cell dividing, and descended. Mara found herself surrounded by Lifelights. A glance at Sebastian showed the same story. They brushed against her lightly, the sensation a fizzing caress. She became aware of her hair lifting around her, spreading out through the air, as if charged with static. Looking back at Sebastian, Mara had the urge to laugh. His rich brown hair stood to attention.

Their eyes met and all thoughts of laughter died.

As the Lifelights continued to pulse about them, Mara was aware of a deeper connection forming.

Flashes of information streamed from her subconscious. Multiple moments in time, each one a variation of this one flowed across her mind's eye.

Her body temperature rose sharply, as heat surged its way out of her mind, falling through her from head to toe. Her heart rate increased as her lungs pulled in air, in a frantic bid to cool her down. She shivered violently.

In the next moment the Lifelights brightened further, effectively blinding her. All she could see was pulsating light, all she could feel was heat infusing her. Both were linked, in perfect synchronisation. The twin assaults on her senses left Mara with no room to manoeuvre. Then there was sound, and something akin to white noise flooded her ears.

She became trapped, cocooned from the world she knew. She could do nothing but exist, blind, deaf and dumb. The heat evaporated the moisture in her mouth and throat, until no sound could escape.

Mara's trust in the Lifelights was all consuming. Awe blossomed within her. The voice, Sebastian, had not belonged to them. This did.

For some reason, Sebastian's presence had triggered the thing she craved most. A deeper, closer connection with the only constants she'd ever known.

She didn't understand it.

She didn't care.

Joy was the closest equal to the emotion that now surged through Mara. It ripped through her soul, leaving wonder in its wake, the bright light and white noise intensifying for an immeasurable amount of time.

Then everything began to fade, as her mind overloaded on sensation.

Mara heard herself scream in denial. She wanted the connection back.

* * * *

Sebastian was shouting. It was inconsiderate of him at best and downright evil at worst. Why couldn't he just leave her alone?

"Mara? Are you awake?"

"No."

Someone squeezed her, too tight, "Please, Mara, come and keep me company...."

She opened her eyes for a second, shutting them quickly on a whine of pain.

The Lifelights were still there, glowing brightly. Too brightly.

Sebastian was laughing now, "I saw that. Come on, pretty girl, time to rejoin the land of the living. These Lifelights of yours are getting a tad aggressive; as if this is *my* fault!"

Mara scowled, and still refused to open her eyes.

"It is your fault. You're the one who wanted to meet them." She'd deliberately reverted to verbal communication, in the hope it annoyed him.

"I suppose you're right."

Well that was a shock. Had Sebastian just *agreed* with her?

Mara opened her eyes again.

She was still in the hallway, but arranged across Sebastian's knee. He was sitting on the floor, his back resting against the solidity of the front door. The Lifelights were crowded around them. They zoomed about in agitated groups, their light fluctuating in random patterns. Each fly-past raised goose bumps along her skin.

"What are they doing?" She asked, puzzled.

"What makes you think I know? At a guess I'd say they're worrying themselves dizzy. You've been unconscious for over five minutes."

Mara giggled, which was slightly worrying in itself. Was she getting hysterical?

He was right. It did look like the Lifelights were worrying themselves dizzy.

She sighed, and tried to get up, only to find that he refused to let go. Not having the energy to fight, she contented herself with a shift in position. She looked up at the Lifelights.

"It's okay. I'm here. Nothing's wrong." She hoped the whispered words would calm them.

The Lifelights stopped, hanging in mid-air.

Mara smiled in relief, but it was short-lived. As she continued to shrug off the darkness, her mind grew more aware. Dread began to build. Something was wrong.

It was as if her emotions and those of the Lifelights had aligned.

The connection was nothing like the one she shared with Sebastian, but she could sense the Lifelights' feelings. They were distressed and there was something else… guilt?

She watched them with suspicion.

"What is it, my Mara? You've grown tense... Relax." Even expressing concern, Sebastian made it sound like an order.

"They're up to something." Mara explained.

"Are you sure?" This time Sebastian spoke aloud. He sounded surprised. "What makes you think that?"

Mara twisted round, so that she could look up at him, "Because something happened to me when we came into the cottage tonight, and now I seem to be much more aware of what they're 'thinking'. Does that make sense?"

Sebastian looked serious, “You can understand them?”

“Not understand them, exactly. It’s more a feeling I have, as if something bad is about to happen…” Mara trailed off as she tried to get a better grip on what she was ‘feeling’. Then it came to her.

It slid across her mind like an oil slick.

“Oh no…”

She began to struggle, frustrated by the tight hold that Sebastian had on her. She had to get up, had to stop them… but it was too late.

The Lifelights began to move again, drawing her gaze.

They spun upwards, into a pillar of light. Faster and faster, until they began to blur at the edges, leaving comet trails in their wake.

And then they began to disappear.

It was like watching bulbs pop. Two blue, two green, two red, a gold and a silver… they vanished from sight without a sound.

Mara struggled harder for a moment, before she collapsed back with a sob. Tears ran unhindered down her cheeks.

Her grief echoed around the hallway. This couldn’t be happening.

She rocked forward where she sat, arms outstretched, hands and fingers straining, as she fought to escape Sebastian’s grip.

“No… no, please, let me go. Where have they gone? Why would they leave me? What did I do?” Again, grief was given voice. It scattered the remaining Lifelights, as they sped back to her side, regrouping around her.

She felt Sebastian’s hands rubbing at her arms, his voice low and gentle as he spoke to her, but she couldn’t make sense of the words.

She couldn't do this; couldn't lose those closest to her.

She'd never survive the pain, not again. Hadn't her parents, grandparents, been enough?

As Mara abandoned herself to disbelief, denial and misery, the Lifelights took over. They brightened, blinding her, cutting off everything except the sound of Sebastian's voice in her mind and the touch of his hands.

"Calm down, Mara, this isn't what it seems. Trust me..."

Being knocked out by a mind overload had been bad enough the first time. The second time wasn't any better.

Mara's last thought was, *"Don't you bloody dare!"* As she realised, belatedly, what they were up to.

* * * *

She wasn't sure how long they'd kept her out for this time, but it hadn't helped.

"They left me!"

The words were a cry of anguish in her mind. Comfort came instantly, as an arm wrapped itself around her waist. She was hugged tightly, pulled back against a warm body.

"No, my Mara, they didn't. Well, not exactly. This is going to take some explaining."

That got her attention. Her eyes shot open and she tensed. Bit by bit, the details of where she was and who she was with started to come back to her.

The hallway had been exchanged for the living room. She was laid on her side facing the back of the large, ancient sofa that overpowered the tiny room.

The Lifelights were clearly visible, arranged along the sofa back, their soft light comforting in the surrounding gloom.

Mara had lain like this numerous times in her life, enjoying alone time with them.

And therein lay the crucial difference. This time there was someone with her, her body cradled against his. In any other circumstance, it would be nice, better than nice. Mara's skin heated, as her imagination came up with a series of highly detailed, sensual scenarios, all featuring the sofa in various… positions. Where had *that* come from? It really wasn't appropriate, especially now, when Sebastian was the man sharing the sofa with her. She could only hope he hadn't been listening in.

"Now why would you hope that, my Mara? A vivid imagination is a wonderful thing."

Mara's breath caught in her throat as she felt herself being moved, rolled onto her back.

Sebastian's face appeared above her, his chin resting on the palm of one hand as he propped himself up. His arm left her waist, his hand tracing along her cheek and neck, before coming to rest on her collarbone.

Yep, something had definitely changed. *Perhaps Jennie's outlook is catching?* Mara was conscious of every point of contact between them and she could definitely see him as a treat to be savoured. The feeling of intimacy grew as she looked up at him.

His eyes glimmered in the near darkness, his features illuminated by the glow from the Lifelights. He bent his head, brushing her lips with his. It was an undemanding caress, layered with tension. The sort, she quickly realised, that made her want to grab him and have done with it.

"Hello, my darling. How are you feeling? Better?"

Mara gave a small nod of assent. She was having trouble focusing on Sebastian's words, hyper aware of his lips. So close. And that hand, where exactly was that going? The pads of his fingers smoothed across her skin, his fingers exploring further south. They grazed the swell of her breasts. Responsive ripples flowed out from where he touched her, spreading through her body.

This was wrong… right… no, wrong… maybe.

"Sebastian!!"

A chuckle sounded and the hand stilled.

"How right you are, my Mara. This is neither the time nor the place for courting... or seducing. Explanations are called for.

"Care to offer me that coffee now?" He touched her cheek softly, and then rolled over, rising to his feet. He reached out his hand towards her.

The Lifelights flew upwards as she accepted his offer of help.

The Lifelights minus eight, she reminded herself. The sense of loss ran deep, polarised by her inability to understand why.

Mara's mind was a scrambled mess of arousal, grief, disbelief and outright denial. She didn't hold out much hope that Sebastian could explain this to her. He'd only met the Lifelights tonight, but she couldn't think of a better alternative. She'd let him try.

Maybe he'd seen something she hadn't, something that happened whilst she was unconscious.

Decision made, she led the way through to the kitchen.

The cottage had a surreal atmosphere to it. Mara shrugged it off. Obviously the shedding of too many tears had left her both weak *and* fanciful. Her face felt tight under its layer of salt.

She blinked uncomfortably as the kitchen light came on, and then got busy, ignoring Sebastian. She filled the kettle and laid out everything she needed. Instant coffee, teaspoon, cups and milk (for her) were soon sitting on the worktop. Routine had rescued her many times over the years, helping her to bury unwelcome emotions and memories.

It would rescue her now.

As the kettle boiled, Mara turned to rest against the kitchen units and looked directly at Sebastian, who had sat down on one of the chairs by the kitchen table and was currently staring at his legs, stretched out in front of him.

"It wasn't an accident that you came into The Tea Cosy, was it?" She asked.

Sebastian looked up at her.

"No. I've already told you that."

Mara frowned, casting her mind back through their previous conversations and 'mind talking'. Then she remembered. He had told her.

Still feeling confused, she turned back to the worktop when she heard the kettle click off and began spooning instant coffee into the cups. A minute later she crossed over to the kitchen table and settled herself down onto another of the chairs, careful to keep the table between them. It was galling to realise that, even after the upheaval of the evening, she had the urge to launch herself at him, beg him to kiss her again and blot out everything else.

She pushed a cup of black coffee towards him.

Silence reigned as they stared at each other.

Mara cleared her throat before speaking, "You've said some strange things since I've known you, Sebastian. Your comment about waiting nineteen years, for 'this', topped the lot though. What did you mean?"

Sebastian took a sip of his drink and shrugged. "I meant what I said. I've been waiting to meet you, be with you, for nineteen years. I've known of you, been talking to you, for all of that time. You've only had the ability to hear me for the last three days."

"What's so special about the last three days?" She asked.

"You've only been mature enough to hear me for the last three days, Mara. Our species is a little strange like that. Within each cycle, the women come of age and gain access to their gifts on or around their Twenty Second birthdays."

Mara took a huge gulp of her coffee and immediately regretted it, the too hot liquid scalding her tongue and throat.

"What do you mean by 'our species' and 'gifts'? You're as human as I am Sebastian Oran." She paused, as a thought occurred to her, "Oh, please, don't tell me you're an escaped mental patient with a thing for fast cars?"

Sebastian lost the battle to keep a straight face. He grinned, and Mara buried her face in her hands.

What had she got herself into? She'd known that there was more to this man than met the eye, but she'd never suspected he was unhinged!

"Do you think I'm unhinged when I talk to you like this? Do you think humans talk to each other like this?"

He had a point, but Mara gave in to her stubborn streak anyway. Looking up again, she glared across the table at him.

"Some of them might. There are those who believe they're psychic and they say they can do this kind of thing."

"So you think you and I are psychic humans, do you, Mara?"

"It's possible." She mumbled, feeling mutinous.

Sebastian threw up his hands, as if in surrender.

"Yes, I suppose it is possible. That doesn't explain the Lifelights though. If we're psychic humans, then what are they?"

Mara glared across the table again, "How should I know? Maybe they're ghosts or guardian angels?"

Midway through taking a drink of coffee, Sebastian nearly spat it out again.

"Oh, Mara, I had hoped you'd have more of an open mind about this. Okay, leaving the Lifelights out of this for the moment, at least let me show you that you're special. Please?"

She thought about it, and then agreed with a curt nod.

Sebastian relaxed a little, his face softening. *"Here goes then. Mara, you aren't just able to speak telepathically, something that certainly did start on your twenty second birthday, you're also able to harness and manipulate energy; electricity in particular."*

Mara snorted. "Rubbish!"

Unperturbed by the interruption, Sebastian continued. *"If it's rubbish, then how did you manage to bake your cakes perfectly at the café this morning, when you forgot to switch the oven on? And how did you boil the kettle just now, without actually plugging it in?"*

Having opened her mouth to laugh at the suggestion about the oven, Mara's head whipped round when he mentioned the kettle. Her stomach lurched.

She'd always had a 'thing' about unplugging her electrical appliances whilst she was at work…

Sure enough, as her eyes followed the electric lead from the kettle, she saw the plug resting on the worktop, nowhere near the socket on the wall above it.

She stared at it in horror, vaguely aware that the Lifelights were piling in around her. Their movements were agitated.

Turning back to look at Sebastian, she was surprised to find him not watching her, but the Lifelights. His expression was thoughtful.

"Maybe I shouldn't have said that the Lifelights 'liked' me. It would be truer to say that they 'recognised' me."

Mara didn't know what to say to that.

The Lifelights still surrounded her. Turning her hands palm up, some of them nestled there. Mara smiled, until she remembered the kettle. She touched a finger against the side of her coffee mug.

"There is no way that an unplugged kettle can boil water. So how come our coffees are hot?" She asked.

"Because you provided the electrical charge, you did it unconsciously, as you were born to.

"I have the same gift, Mara. It's what drew us together in the beginning, so many years ago. The attraction never lessens. It's what draws us together now."

The look Sebastian gave her was intense. Mara dropped her gaze and thought about what he'd said. She couldn't argue with a disconnected plug.

"You're telling me that neither of us are human, Sebastian? If that's true, what are we?"

He didn't reply.

The silence stretched out, until Mara looked up.

Sebastian was staring at her, his expression grave.

A second later his body shimmered, bright particles exploding outwards. They ripped his body apart and reformed it in front of her.

His chair was empty now, except for the four bright lights hovering above it.

No wonder the Lifelights were grouped in fours.

CHAPTER 7

As there was no way her legs would support her, Mara didn't run. Anyway, this was Sebastian.

A Lifelight.

Like the ones she'd grown up with. It wasn't in her to panic or scream. There were too many positive emotions and memories attached to the sight in front of her.

Out of the four lights, red, blue, green and silver, *his lights*, the silver shone brightest. It figured. That was the colour she'd seen in his eyes.

It all made sense; in a Dr. Seuss kind of way.

"Now what would a nice English girl like you, know about Dr. Seuss?"

The amused question, delivered with more than a hint of arrogance, was pure Sebastian. Mara couldn't help smiling, "*That's for me to know and you to find out Mr. Lifelight Man. Suffice to say, I still have my copy of Sleep Book.*"

She watched as he floated higher, his lights colouring the white ceiling, before he twirled his way across the kitchen. He slipped through the centre of 'her' Lifelights and dipped lower, down towards the kitchen floor. Then he hovered in front of her.

Could a man be beautiful? Sebastian was.

As she stared at him, he changed. His lights merged into a multi-coloured ball, which rapidly expanded. It stretched, gathered mass, reshaped into a recognisable body. The light was re-absorbed, locked beneath skin, hair and, surprisingly, clothes.

He knelt in front of her, his expression a strange mixture of wariness and humour. His hands held hers firmly, as if he expected her to flee the first chance she got. Slowly, he leaned towards her. His voice whispered seductively in her mind.

"You have a copy of Dr. Seuss's Sleep Book? Isn't that the one that says 'This Book is to be Read in Bed'?" He leered at her, *"I'm willing, if you are, gorgeous."*

"Now why does that *not* surprise me?" Mara's laughter filled the kitchen, "Give me a break. No suggestive comments allowed. This is going to take some getting used to, you know. You've just told me you're not human!"

"Only half right, my Mara. I've just told you that we're not human."

She'd forgotten that bit.

"As far as *I'm* concerned, the Jury's still out." She held up her hand when he looked ready to argue, "First things first. Who are you?" She asked.

Abruptly, Sebastian stopped trying to speak. He stared at her, a small frown appearing. It seemed that the answer wasn't going to be straight forward.

He sighed, gave her hands a squeeze and then rose to his feet, sitting back down on the chair opposite her. Pulling his abandoned coffee mug towards him, he contemplated the steaming contents.

Watching him, Mara's natural humour began to surface. If what he'd said was true, it looked like she could bin the thermos flasks. Maybe the hot water bottles too.

The silence went on for so long, it came as a shock when Sebastian finally spoke.

"I'm the same person who walked into The Tea Cosy three days ago. I just have more of a connection to you than you realised. Hopefully, that makes you think more of me, not less."

"Don't bet on it." Mara crossed her arms, "I want details, Sebastian. I'm struggling to understand all this. Up until three days ago I was living a fairly boring life, if you discount the Lifelights. Then you arrive and all hell breaks loose. So you tell me. Why on earth would I want more of that?"

"Because you know, deep down, that you recognise me. You feel the same attraction that I do.

"I've known where you were for nineteen years, Mara. I was fifteen when I first became aware of you, too young to come to you. Knowing that I had to wait... Have you any idea how hard that was for me as a man? Because I was a man then; I've had the knowledge and memories of a man from the moment I was born, trapped in a maturing human body.

"It's the way it is for us.

"I want you, Mara, make no mistake. In every way a human would and more. I want the girl whose soul connected to mine when she was three, crying out in a moment of grief. I want the woman that girl grew into, who is only now becoming aware of what she is. I want the one Lifelight meant for me.

"We belong together."

Mara felt her heart jolt as she listened to Sebastian's words. She allowed her arms to unfold, her hands resting lightly on the very edge of the table. Then she leant forward, every cell in her body responding to the plea in his voice and the pull of his eyes.

But she still needed answers. She knew she'd allowed herself to drift through life, never questioning things. It hadn't even occurred to her to question the presence of the Lifelights.

It was time she started.

"Who are my Lifelights, Sebastian? Who did I lose tonight?"

For a moment she wondered if he'd refuse to answer. Then she heard him.

"Sometimes the questions are simple and the answers are complicated. Can't you come to me without knowing everything? I can tell you, will tell you, but I'd like to know that you trust me. Do you trust me, Mara?"

Trust him. For the first time she realised how hard that was. She'd trusted her grandparents, but they were gone. She trusted Jennie, but that had been earned. She'd *never* trusted anyone purely on instinct. And that was what he was asking from her; a leap of faith.

Mara pulled in a long breath and closed her eyes. There was a part of her that demanded answers to *all* her questions before she considered trusting him. But… would it really be so bad if she let herself *belong*, as he wanted her to?

She didn't open her eyes again until she'd made her decision.

"Yes. I trust you. I can wait a little longer for the answers."

Sebastian's smile was almost as bright as his lights. He went to take her hand across the table, but she held it up as she began to speak again, "And for future reference, don't *ever* misquote Dr. Seuss at me again. You'll lose my respect forever."

There was something about his laughter, the way she could hear it inside and out, that sent shivers of pleasure down her back.

"Noted, my Mara; I was just going with the theme. I didn't think you'd notice."

She shook her head, "I noticed, and that's no excuse."

"I suppose not," he acknowledged, before lapsing into silence, staring at her with that intense expression that never failed to set her pulse racing.

"What?" She asked, trying to keep her tone light.

"I was just wondering... *what excuse would I need to kiss you again?"*

For a moment, Mara was speechless.

To Sebastian, speechlessness apparently equalled an invitation. He was in front of her before she'd realised he'd moved, pulling her up out of her chair.

Arousal, so new to her, was instant.

He lowered his head, covering her mouth with his, increasing the pressure until she responded. Opening her lips, her tongue willingly mimicked his. With sweeping strokes, deep and soft, they learned each other's touch and taste. His hands came up to frame her face, gliding along her cheeks and into her hair. Fingers massaged the sensitive skin of her scalp in slow, languid motions.

Mara was aware of a rising urgency. It swirled from mind to mind. Her need to understand was answered by his need to show her what existed between them. And with each new contact, each stroke of lips and hands, she could feel the energy growing.

Right now, she could believe she was Lifelight.

Sharp electricity pushed outwards, welling up from somewhere inside her, rippling across her skin to meet Sebastian's own unique charge, crackling and popping as they combined. Their skin became flushed with heat, as the power jumped between them. It raced deep into her abdomen, where it centred itself into a heavy mass, knotting her muscles with an aching need.

The Lifelights went mad. They whirled around them, leaving tiny trails of coloured light in their wake. Mara's heart raced and she began to feel dizzy, as her body strove to match the frenzy of the Lifelights and the throb of power inside her. If she hadn't been held, anchored to Sebastian, she'd have fallen.

Here was a man who made her knees weak. A bubble of humour rose with the thought. Jennie would be proud.

It had never occurred to her that sexual arousal could generate this kind of electrical energy. As the kiss continued even the air around them, agitated by the Lifelights, glowed with the excess energy their bodies were producing.

Surely, she thought, this couldn't continue? They'd burn up before they even contemplated moving on from this kiss.

A laugh of pure, male, amusement lightly touched Mara's mind as Sebastian finally raised his head. His expression was one of satisfaction as he looked down at her, his hands still gently massaging her scalp. All she could do was gaze back at him, her eyes heavy lidded, her muscles relaxed, the throbbing inside her refusing to dissipate

"If only you knew how much I want you, my Mara. Right now." Sebastian's eyes brightened, even as he made a visible effort to slow his breathing. *"I remember the pleasure, and the passion. But we must be careful. This much energy will not go unnoticed. That can be dangerous for us."*

Mara frowned, confusion making an unwelcome intrusion into her thoughts. *"I don't understand. Isn't this how it's supposed to be? Am I doing something wrong?"* The Lifelights were slowing, their light softer, almost diffused.

Sebastian shook his head as he moved position. He pulled Mara down onto her original seat, cradled her on his knee, her head on his shoulder as he leaned her into him, his arms around her. She felt him rest his chin on the top of her head, his breath ruffling her hair. "Oh, Mara," he whispered, "How am I going to find the words? This is never easy, explaining our history. There's so much you need to know and so little time."

She stiffened. "What do you mean?"

Sebastian's fingers stroked down the length of her arm, circling her wrist gently as his thumb moved in lazy circles across her palm. The sensuous touch produced a tingle of electricity and Mara shivered. Aware that Sebastian was searching for the right words, she waited patiently, enjoying the subtle flow of power.

Finally he connected with her, *"You saw how I transformed my body from human in appearance to my natural state?"* She nodded. *"That's something that you too will be able to do."*

Mara felt a shiver of anticipation, *"Really? You're sure?"*

He must have caught her excitement. Relief filled his mind. *"Yes, it's part of who you are. We're a species made from energy; it drives everything about us, including our change from one form to another. All you need is the right sort of energy and a large enough source of it. Your body will do the rest. A chain reaction will start, that ends with the first change. Once that happens, you'll be able to learn from the experience and will know how to replicate the surge of power for yourself. You'll be able to change at will, just as I did."*

Sebastian sounded hesitant, as if there was something else he wanted to tell her, but didn't know how to.

Smiling to herself, Mara quickly sifted through what he *had* said, before deliberately making her mind blank, as she'd done at the café. "That sounds simple enough – so where do I find the initial power?"

She had a pretty good idea, after that kiss. She was going to enjoy this and she even got to make Sebastian sweat a little.

He hesitated before replying. “Well, err; there are a number of ways to get the level of energy required. The heat energy found in Magma would be enough, though that involves getting rather too close to a volcano. Not a good idea. Then there’s the kinetic energy of the sea or the energy created by a storm. Unfortunately these can be difficult to control, especially for a newly matured female.”

Mara nodded. She continued to blank her mind. Not an easy thing to do when trying not to laugh. “So, what’s the best source for someone like me, Sebastian?” Her voice was as sweetly innocent as she could make it.

There was a long silence. Mara could feel Sebastian’s chin, worrying at the top of her head, the pressure of his jaw bone rubbing backwards and forwards for several moments before he finally replied. “I don’t think there’s an easy way to say this. The best trigger for a first change is… sexual energy.”

“Oh.” Mara struggled, but ultimately failed to stop her amusement filling the single word. In seconds it had spread, her body shaking with laughter as she tipped her head back to look at him. “Well, that’s an original way to proposition a woman.”

“What is?” Sebastian looked puzzled.

“Come back with me babe…” Mara waggled her eyebrows for effect, “and I’ll show you such a good time, you’ll burst into balls of light!” Her laughter burst free when she caught sight of his expression, “Oh, god, the look on your face is priceless!”

“You’ll pay for this...” Sebastian did his best to sound fierce, but his smile came back swiftly when he heard her reply.

"I'm counting on it, if I want to make that change any time soon."

Sebastian looked like he was tempted to take her up on the offer immediately. He began to bend his head towards hers.

Why did she have to be the sensible one?

She placed a hand on his chest. It was best to calm things down; sexy mind talk was not an option. "Slow down Mr. Lifelight Man; first, don't you have something to tell me? Don't think I missed that bit about us being in danger. Not to mention the million or so other questions I have lined up for you."

Her question had the desired, if disappointing, outcome. Sebastian stopped abruptly, his face becoming a solemn mask, as he spoke out loud. "You're right; there are things you need to know, things that can't wait. Accept this though; we've already started certain changes within your body, your reaction to me saw to that. Our time is now limited.

"You will start to produce and attract power at a phenomenal rate. This is your body preparing you for the change, when every cell will be wrenched apart and converted into pure energy. If we don't find a suitable place for you to attempt the change soon, your body will become overloaded."

Mara didn't like the sound of that, "Isn't here a suitable place?"

"I'm afraid not," Sebastian replied

"Why?" Mara couldn't think what the problem was. Okay, so maybe they'd have to send the Lifelights out the room. If they were really like him, then there was no way she was having an audience for what he obviously had in mind. But her nearest neighbours were three miles away. What more did he want?

"Complete isolation. There are those who hunt us, Mara. By changing in front of you, so close to traceable power lines, I've already placed you in danger. As I said before, there is so much you need to know."

"I don't understand." Mara tried to grasp what he'd just said. "*Why would anyone want to hunt us?*"

Laughter, this time tinged with bitterness, flooded her mind. *"Such an innocent, and how I wish you could stay like that. Didn't you know? Lifelights are a hot commodity. If just one of us were caught, a lot of people would be very happy indeed."*

Mara still didn't understand.

Sebastian pulled her closer, protectively, before continuing, "We're all in danger, every Lifelight, because we *are* energy. Something this world is addicted to.

"The amount of energy produced by a single Lifelight, in a single change, is enough to power the city of London for a day. Just think what could be done with ten, twenty, a hundred of us. Just think what could be done with an entire species.

"It doesn't matter how many renewables my company, or others like it, come up with. There will always be those who want the easy option and we, my darling, are it."

The horror of the world Sebastian described was all too real. Mara did indeed have a vivid imagination, and she cringed at the picture it painted for her. Her muscles protested as every fibre locked into place. "But surely, if we offered to help, people would work with us. Isn't it better to get results from co-operation, rather than force?"

Sebastian's denial was instant and harsh, "I only wish I had your faith, but I do not." He looked down at her, his expression softening, until it was almost tender. He ran a soothing hand along her arm and spoke directly to her mind. *"No, we must never allow our true natures to be discovered. We cannot take the chance. We are more than sacks of coal or barrels of oil."*

His words unravelled the last of Mara's control. Sobs shook her as she looked at the Lifelights crowded around them. She stared into the beauty of Sebastian's eyes, sparking with the very energy that he'd described as a threat to them.

He allowed her to cry, rocking her, as a storm of weeping and denial took hold. Keenly aware of the arms holding her, Mara wished that she had better access to his mind. What was he thinking?

"Of you, my Mara," Sebastian whispered the words in her mind, "*We have little time. You have yet to change and I can feel the energy your body is producing, the way you draw it to you from every source. We need to leave and I wish that I didn't have to ask you to, when this has been your home for so long."*

"But we have no choice, do we?" Mara replied, the tears sliding down her cheeks.

After several long minutes, Sebastian stood, cradling her against his chest. He walked steadily through the cottage and outside.

Mara looked back at the place that had been her home for nineteen years. She understood, without words, that they were leaving for good. She could see the Lifelights. It was the first time she'd seen them outside the walls of the cottage. They gathered under the porch, their light brightening. Then they disappeared, as quickly and silently as the others.

Mara cried even harder, burrowing against the warmth of Sebastian's shoulder as he lowered her into the car seat and pulled the belt around her. Then she began to laugh, hysteria edging the sound. *"If I'm really a Lifelight and can transform into nothing but energy, why are you putting a seat belt on me? How could a crash kill me? How could one kill my parents?"*

Sebastian leaned forward to brush Mara's lips with a teasing, feather light, kiss. *"I'm fastening you in, my Mara, because you have yet to master the change. Without that you are fragile, as breakable as any human.*

"As for your parents, that's a story I need time to tell. Just know this, you never really lost them."

CHAPTER 8

I'm a Lifelight?

I don't even know what that means. Not really.

They must have been travelling for hours. Darkness had been replaced by daylight.

Mara opened her eyes wide, shrugging off the remnants of a fitful sleep.

She twisted her head to stare at the car's driver. "Sebastian?"

He glanced across at her, not looking in the least tired. She supposed that was understandable. A human would be tired.

"Yes, my Mara?"

"Umm, could we *not* do the mind talking for a bit? I think this is a conversation I need to have out loud."

For a moment silence filled the car, before he nodded in agreement.

Now what?

She flicked through the questions that teemed inside her head.

"You keep saying things about knowing me before, hinting that we've been together for a long time. So let's start there. How old are you, Sebastian?"

"The same age as you. In fact, the same age as every Lifelight on the planet."

Mara let that sink in. "Okay, not sure how that would work, but I'll take your word for it. How old are we talking here?"

"4.3 billion Years."

Shit.

Sebastian's mouth twitched. "Did you just swear?"

"Err..." she paused, as her mind still grappled with the figure he'd thrown at her. "Yes. It's something I do, if the situation warrants it. This qualifies. You're looking good for your age by the way."

"Thank you, as are you. With regard to the swearing, I'm thinking you'll be doing a lot of that. Next question please."

"What? No... not so fast. I'm still on this one. I mean, how the *hell* can we be 4.3 *billion* years old? That's... incomprehensible, unbelievable." She took a breath before continuing, "How can every Lifelight be the same age? Don't we die? Don't we have kids? Exactly how long have we known each other?"

Sebastian gave her a look of approval, "That's more like it. Okay, pay attention, Miss Mara. This is Lifelights 101.

"We're 4.3 billion years old because that's when we were created. We were birthed by energy, the same energy that shaped the Universe, the Solar System, the Earth and the Moon. You've heard of the Big Bang Theory? Well that's how it was for us. We're not sure what the catalyst was, maybe a violent meteor strike or a shift in the Earth's mantle, but one moment we weren't there and the next we were. We don't die, because energy doesn't die, but we do convert. We started out as simple sparks of raw energy, with little understanding of the world we were born into, and have evolved our intelligence and society over time. We don't procreate. Not in the sense you mean. There is the same number of Lifelights on Earth today as there was at the moment of our creation. As for how long we've known each other…" Sebastian grinned at her, "3 billion years, give or take a few."

Bloody hell

"You're swearing again."

"And you're awfully smug."

"I never denied that."

"So… 3 billion years you say? This is a committed relationship then?" Mara couldn't stop her smile, as Sebastian laughed.

"You bet. Of course the twenty plus years of separation that come with each cycle, is a bit of a bummer. Absence may make the heart grow fonder, my love, but its hell on the libido."

Mara sputtered, "Aren't I worth the wait?"

"Do you think I'd have stuck around for 3 billion years if you weren't?"

"Touché. You know, I don't have a clue what these cycles are all about, but I'm going to save those questions for now. My head feels ready to explode."

"I understand. This is always a difficult time for you, Mara."

Silence again, as she settled herself back and thought about everything she had learned. It was several minutes before she spoke.

"Where are we?" She asked. The sun was high in the sky, so it must be close to midday, but nothing about the landscape was familiar.

"Scotland." Sebastian replied.

"Scotland!"

Mara sat bolt upright, "But… what about my job, what about Jennie?"

A few hours ago she couldn't have cared less where she was headed or for how long, but suddenly she needed to know that her friend would be okay. That she was safe.

Sebastian reached out his hand to rub the back of hers. His touch immediately soothed as his voice calmed her from the inside. *"Stop panicking. There are things called cell phones remember? I contacted Jennie whilst you were resting. I have to say, she was shocked when I explained that you could no longer work for her. Not to mention suspicious. She initially accused me of abducting you... but I think we've got that sorted now. I've arranged for temporary staff to cover the work at the café until she can hire someone else."*

"You have?" That surprised her. She knew that he was a business man, but she hadn't expected such thoughtful efficiency.

He chuckled, "Well, when I say that I arranged for temporary staff, it might be more truthful to say that Alexa arranged it. Actually, it was her that managed to reassure Jennie too. She's an excellent P.A."

Mara allowed her eyes to rest on him thoughtfully. The feeling of belonging, that she'd always craved, was growing with each mile they travelled. It was like being wrapped in a warm, invisible blanket. Not so welcome but nonetheless there, was a knotted, heavy sensation deep inside her. It ached.

In an effort to distract herself, she turned her head to look back at the scenery they passed. She was becoming far too fond of staring at Sebastian's profile, especially his mouth.

"Where are you taking me?" She asked.

"To Slioch, one of the Munroes, also known as 'the hill of the spear'. It's one of the rare places that the Lifelights have made their own; a sanctuary. There are caves there that can shelter us. It will be the perfect place for you to attempt the change."

Mara wondered how the change would feel and what it would entail. The ache inside her had intensified. She spread her free hand over her stomach, where it was most noticeable. Warmth was spreading through her, from skin to bone and everywhere in between. Looking down she saw a glow surrounding her hand. A soft aura outlined each finger. It fluctuated every so often, as if responding to the movement she could feel rolling beneath her skin. Without explanation, she knew that this was the energy Sebastian had told her about.

It was building in strength. Preparing her. It was starting to seriously hurt.

The quick glances that Sebastian threw her way were growing more concerned. She decided not to ask too many questions. If she was about to spontaneously combust, she'd rather not know about it.

The next four hours blurred, as Mara battled a rising tide of pain and heat. She found herself drifting in and out of consciousness, only rousing herself when Sebastian squeezed her shoulder and whispered in her ear. "We're here. How're you feeling?"

Squinting out of the car window, she shrugged. "Okay I guess. It hurts, but it's bearable."

"Really?" He sounded relieved and visibly relaxed.

Stuff that. Maybe the truth would be better. Mara was beginning to feel pissed-off. Now was not the time for him to switch off that amazing telepathy of his.

She opened her mind and pushed every sensation into his. Watching him squirm in discomfort, she spoke as calmly as she was able. "No. It hurts like blazes and if it gets much worse, swearing will be the least of your problems. Grievous bodily harm and screaming will be distinct possibilities."

As her pain continued to batter him, Sebastian paled. His movements were urgent as he left the car and pulled open the passenger door beside her.

The light was already dimming, as evening began to draw in. There wasn't another person in sight. Heather filled moor land stretched out around them. Only the surrounding mountains dared to break the wide vista. Their heavily wooded slopes cocooned the valley.

"I'm afraid we have to walk from here." Sebastian said, lifting her into his arms.

The air outside the car was crisply cold. As it touched her overheated skin, Mara shivered violently. Her body immediately compensated, raising her temperature higher. Sweat soaked her clothes.

She looked up at him, her smile more of a grimace now. *"Not feeling too good right now."*

Sebastian nodded, his eyes trained on her left hand as it clutched at the fabric covering her abdomen. Following his gaze, she saw that the aura around her hand shone even more brightly.

"You're very close. I don't think we'll reach our final destination before the change needs to take place."

He sounded worried.

Mara was past caring. She hardly noticed as they turned away from the car, moving towards the mountains. She did spare a thought for how impressive they were. Majestic and austere, their towering peaks were silhouetted against a richly coloured sunset. She allowed the sight to hold her in awe, only vaguely aware that they were moving faster than should be possible. Sebastian's feet barely skimmed the ground.

The air blew about her face, like a caress. The heat that had started out just below her hand radiated outwards in pulsing waves.

Her heart rate spiked suddenly, racing hard and fast in her chest.

"Sebastian!" She cried out, as intense pain sliced through her.

His reaction was instantaneous. He stopped abruptly, his head swinging from side to side as he assessed their position.

They hadn't reached the caves of Slioch. Empty moor land surrounded them, their only witnesses the mountains themselves.

She knew they were out of time. Their choices were limited.

What now?

He placed her on her feet, always gentle, and then cupped her head in his hands. His eyes stared into hers.

"It's time, my Mara. Should anyone see this, let's pray that they mistake us for the Northern Lights. You're going to be incandescent, my love."

The last two words were spoken in quiet veneration. They reverberated through her as he lowered his head to hers. Their kiss re-kindled the desire that had touched her at the cottage.

She felt the instant chemistry, as the energy within her responded to his touch. It raged between them. Every particle of her body burned with the heat of it.

One of Sebastian's hands pushed through her hair. It cradled her scalp as the other slowly caressed her cheek, then neck. It continued lower to tug at the buttons of her blouse, before pushing the silky fabric aside.

Her bra was dispensed with a minute later. Breasts bared, she felt his fingers stroke across them, adding to the sensitivity of her skin, and her breath caught. Her desire was mixed with impatience. When their mouths separated she moaned in annoyance.

Where does he think he's going?

Not far, apparently. Sebastian's lips dipped, to trail along the column of her throat, following the path that his fingers had taken earlier. She moaned again as his mouth closed around her breast, even as his hand moved on; downwards to the waistband of her skirt. Clever fingers dealt quickly with the fastening until it pooled on the floor, her underwear beside it.

Hmm, he's done that before.

His touch elicited a sharp-edged sting, an electrical charge that built inside her, merging with the pleasure.

She felt herself being lifted, moved. Moss and heather cushioned her back, bending around her without discomfort. Her fever slick skin welcomed the coolness of the vegetation brushing against it.

Heat roared through her. Sebastian's mouth and hands were exploring every inch of her body, expertly massaging, spreading the heat from cell to cell. She could feel herself losing control. When he left her for the briefest of moments, her eyes and mouth pleaded for his return, unashamed.

Then he was back, rising above her. Naked now. The silver in his eyes blazed, as his mind demanded her acceptance of him.

Her heart hammered at the sight of him. She froze, her eyes widening as fear of the unknown gripped her for a split second.

"Let go, my Mara. Embrace what you are. Give yourself wholly to me."

The words were compelling, their message echoing through her mind. She'd heard them before. Her body arched upwards in automatic response, allowing him to take possession. He thrust into her body and mind, sharing his visions of other times and other places.

Something tore free, as raw heat burned along her limbs, threatening to consume everything in its path. The pulsing mass of tension that had been inside her all day exploded outwards, pleasure and pain searing her flesh in equal measure.

For a moment she was lost, carried away by feelings

that were beyond description. But then the tension began to build again, as quickly as it was released, pushing her higher.

She could hear Sebastian's voice again, as his body continued to move in hers *"Let go, my Mara. Give up this body. Allow yourself to be free."*

For one glorious moment, her eyes locked with his and she felt herself truly fly. Her eyes stretched impossibly wide, as she watched him let go at the same moment. Concentrated energy surged forward, igniting the wild power inside her until it became an unstoppable conflagration.

Sebastian's face blurred and shifted in front of her. Then, before she could respond, before she could think about being frightened, she too reached the limits of her control. Energy ripped its way out of her, transforming into brilliant light.

She came apart.

Disintegrated.

* * * *

"I feel strange, Sebastian." Her voice sounded odd, far away.

Her body felt odd too; weightless.

She opened her eyes and blinked. Everything was bathed in a golden glow. She could see with perfect clarity, in minute detail, but no Sebastian.

"That's normal, my Mara, for the first change. You were magnificent. I never tire of the emotions you share with me when the energy takes us. You are as glorious as ever."

She felt an urge to giggle, something she'd rarely done before meeting him, *"I'm glorious?"*

"Oh yes, my Mara. Let me show you."

Finally, she saw him; he came from behind her, his

light appearing otherworldly. She moved to follow him and found that she could glide effortlessly over the ground. As he picked up the pace, she could keep up with him, moving faster and faster. She passed through the tiniest of gaps between rock and branch, flew over the mountain slopes and peaks with ease, until they came to an expanse of darkened, mirror like water.

"Lochan Fada." Sebastian breathed his voice reverent.

As the two of them hovered above the blackened surface, Mara looked down and stopped. She could see herself. She was there, reflected in the water. Sebastian by her side. *"I look different to you."* She murmured.

"Of course, you are younger, and far brighter because of it."

"It's not just that though, is it? Why are my colours different? Why is one of my lights gold, where yours is silver?" She was puzzled, although she knew that the Lifelights at her cottage had appeared different too.

"The silver light indicates a male of our species, whilst the gold belongs to our females. When we fuse, the two lights and the slightly different ways that we control energy complement each other."

"Fuse?"

"Lifelights have four states, Mara. Hidden, change, natural and fuse. In your human guise you are hidden, you've just experienced the change and you're now in your natural state. The final state, Fuse, is the act of intimacy between Lifelights whilst in their natural form." Sebastian's voice had become softer, more sensuous.

His lights drifted closer.

Feeling suddenly unsure, Mara looked down at their reflections. His lights were so close to hers. They almost touched.

What would happen, if that last gap was crossed?

Excitement made her breath falter, or maybe it was just lust.

"Why don't we find out, my Mara?"

Sebastian's voice rippled along nerve endings, persuasive, tempting.

"Yes, why don't we?"

Caution fled as she pushed towards him with a burst of speed, her natural reserve obliterated by the heat of the moment.

As their lights touched, their conscious minds fused. Their colours mixed, the tone changing, concentrating, in brightness and density. All emotion, the ability to 'feel', folded in on itself, imploding to a point of complete unity.

Then the heat returned, building inside them. It rushed along synaptic connections, joining their memories. Past and present collided, burning through all resistance to complete the alchemy. Their combined power pushed their energy and emotions into a violent reversal, a shockwave, a superheated race between information and sensation, to the edges of conscious reason.

Nothing could have prepared her for this. They were a super nova.

The blast radiated out across the surface of Lochan Fada, the brilliance doubling, as it reflected off the black water, shooting skywards in a stream of vivid, prismatic colour.

In that instant, everything ceased to exist for Mara; everything except Sebastian and the intimacy of their bodies and minds, their separate identities fusing into one, their souls dissolving in pure, undiluted joy.

CHAPTER 9

She was back in her human form, completely naked and surprisingly comfortable with the fact.

The night air didn't feel cold. A slight breeze brushed against her skin, as soft as a kiss.

Stretched out on the shore of Lochan Fada, they stared up at the star filled sky, their bodies curled close. A microclimate of warmth enveloped them and Sebastian, as naked as she, looked extremely pleased with himself.

He pushed up on one elbow so that he could look down at her, his smile indulgent as he reached out to cup her chin.

His thumb traced her lips, gliding across the contours.

It felt delicious.

He nuzzled and kissed her shoulder, her neck, as his hand softly caressed her breast.

"How I've missed you, my Mara. As reunions go, that was pretty spectacular; wouldn't you agree? Never mind feeling the Earth move, it's a wonder we didn't set it on fire."

"We nearly did."

"True, but 'nearly' isn't something I can feel proud of. I'm competitive by nature. *Want to try again?*"

He sounded so hopeful, she couldn't help laughing. The sound wrapped around them. It flowed from her mind to his.

That amazed her.

How can we be this close?

"We share everything during the fuse state. Do you think an experience like that would leave no change? We're bonded Lifelights. There's no closer relationship, at least, not that I'm aware of."

"And you know everything."

"Exactly; I'm so glad you picked up on that. It's only taken you 3 billion years."

Mara brought her hand up to cover her mouth and coughed. The word 'Bullshit' was still clearly audible.

Sebastian grinned, and leaned in for a kiss.

It seemed that her ability to *feel* had also changed. Before, his touch had caused excited anticipation. *Now* a frisson of electrical charge skated across the surface of her skin before sinking inside her, blissfully heated. She felt like a sponge, being soaked in warm honey.

If this was part of being a Lifelight, she was more than happy not to be human.

She wrapped her arms around Sebastian's neck and pulled him closer.

Unfortunately, the real world failed to disappear, no matter how much she tried to ignore it. There were still questions that needed to be answered. There were others out there, like her, possibly relatives. The inconsistencies between her family history and what Sebastian had already told her crowded her mind, demanding clarification.

Mara stared at the stars again.

She could feel her mind was changing, a subtle shifting of information. It had started the moment she woke up after the fuse state. Her brain had access to a second consciousness.

Sebastian's.

Lying perfectly still, she watched the heavens. Her mind wandered as she came to terms with this latest change. A silent, nonverbal communication was gathering strength, developing in fluency.

It was amazing, awesome, beautiful… and weird.

She knew he could hear her too. This was a two-way path. She sensed him debating with himself, which of her questions to answer first. She could even feel his frustration, that there was no easy way of introducing her to the Lifelights.

Overwhelming all of that though was happiness. He was happy he'd found her, proud that she'd accepted everything he'd told her so far and how quickly. He felt satisfied, a little lethargic, and at the same time was eager to hold her, love her.

He was worried about everything still to come.

Sebastian sighed and took her hand, pulling her up from the ground and wrapping his arms around her. The warmth stayed with them as they stared across Lochan Fada, exploring their new, stronger connection.

Then he bent his head and whispered in her ear. "I'll be right back, my Mara. It's time to finish our journey. The caves of Slioch await us." He paused for a moment, "Don't fret, I'm about to show you another wonder of being a Lifelight."

Puzzled, she turned to face him. She was just in time to see his outline blur. Then he was gone.

She gasped, her eyes searching for him in the surrounding darkness. But there was no sign of him.

Where is he?

She barely had time to form the question, when another blur of movement caught her attention. He was back. Only a foot away from her, fully clothed and with her own clothes slung over one arm.

"What the *hell* was that?"

She wasn't sure she could take much more of this.

Sebastian grinned at her, holding her clothes out like a peace offering.

"What can I say? We are a species that can manipulate energy; including light. It's a handy transport system, especially when we're travelling between continents."

The idea of being able to travel that fast was fascinating. Pushing aside her initial shock, Mara grabbed at her clothes. She shimmied into them, her eyes never leaving Sebastian. Once dressed, she stepped across to him and slipped her hand into his.

It was growing light. The colour of dawn crept across the mountain peaks. Remote as they were, she knew that their time alone could be interrupted at any moment. All it would take was the appearance of eager hill walkers or an intrepid angler. The thought of the caves lured her.

"Show me, Sebastian."

"With pleasure, my love, but first you need to merge your mind with mine."

He was still grinning and she couldn't think what he found so amusing.

"This isn't some sort of kinky foreplay is it?" She asked, suspicious. "*You seem rather taken with the touchy feely stuff and, as I haven't a clue how you travel like that, I'm at a disadvantage. This had better not be a wind-up."*

Sebastian laughed as he caught her in his arms and pulled her against him. He lowered his head, until his mouth was only inches away from hers. *"You're right, I'm VERY taken with the touchy feely stuff, but I promise that this isn't a wind-up. To travel at such speed, you first need to know where you're going. As you cannot yet remember the caves within Slioch, you'll need to merge your mind with mine. That way you can take the details straight from my memories."*

Mara had to admit that this made sense, but she was becoming distracted by the silver that swirled in his eyes; and what was it about his mouth that she found *so* fascinating? He laughed again, the sound vibrating through the muscles of his chest as his eyes flashed brighter.

With a concerted effort, she focused on the task at hand. Staring into his eyes she felt the familiar attraction between them. It was an almost primitive ‘pull’. She relaxed, surrendering without thought, allowing their minds to merge. Following his lead, she allowed him to draw her into his memories.

The caves were stunning, Sebastian’s memory a work of art. Incredibly detailed, it was almost three dimensional in nature, like a hologram. It was also more than visual. Layered within the image, information flashed across her mind.

The caves of Slioch, with their cathedral like proportions, were created from glimmering sandstone and… something else. A substance she didn’t recognise made its presence felt, giving off a subtle energy signature of its own.

The Lifelights had taken a humble natural formation and created a palace of wonders. There were huge rooms and corridors. Pillars of supporting stone had been lovingly shaped and painted, soaring up from a shimmering floor, to a ceiling of gem stone ‘constellations’, set within a lapis lazuli sky. The walls were decorated with murals, depicting the history of the Lifelights, together with hundreds of carved niches. Each one contained candles.

Rocky outcrops, that looked too structured to be completely natural, were dotted throughout the caves. Almost like furniture. Their only decoration was the subtle sparkle of… again, she wasn’t sure. Was that sandstone, or the 'other' she'd sensed? The sides of the structures were rough, whilst their tops had been polished to a, mirror-like shine.

It all looked and felt real. She could almost believe that she was there, deep within Slioch.

"It is done, my love."

Sebastian's gentle whisper shocked her, whirling her out of the fantasy. Blinking and disorientated, she realised that she was still pressed against him. The muted light of early morning had been replaced by another light source.

What is that?

Turning within his arms, she discovered that it was indeed 'done'. They were standing in the centre of the largest of the caves she'd seen through Sebastian's memory.

They'd travelled here in the space of a heartbeat.

She dragged air into her lungs, forcing herself to breath. Strange as all this was, indulging in a panic attack wasn't an option. If she believed everything so far, this place was part of her heritage. A heritage she hadn't even known she possessed.

Her gaze roamed across the glimmering cave walls and higher, to the ceiling above. It should, by rights, have been pitch black within the caves. But it wasn't.

It didn't take her long to realise why. It was the caves themselves. Every surface gave off a soft luminescence. Looking down, she was shocked to realise that she too was adding to the effect. Her skin was giving off a subtle glow, patterns of light dancing across its surface.

Okay, that's freaky. Cool, but definitely freaky.

"Perhaps you'll find this more acceptable?"

Sebastian's hand passed through the air in a graceful arc. The candles that lined the cave walls flared into life.

Their flickering light and the shadows that danced across the painted walls triggered something within Mara. A sense of wonder and peace spread through her. *Have I really been here before?*

She felt Sebastian's arms tighten around her waist as he bent his head forward, resting his chin on the top of her head.

"Yes. Don't worry, you'll remember eventually."

The candles began to release a heavy perfume; it drifted through the cavern, vaguely floral with a hint of … musk? Mara breathed deeply, enjoying the way that it instantly relaxed her. There was no need for her to be afraid.

"Tell me about the cycles," she whispered.

He didn't answer her immediately; instead he caught hold of her hand and tugged her across the cavern. When they reached the far wall, Mara realised that they were heading for the entrance to a much smaller space, just off the main chamber. Stepping across its threshold, she regarded the interior with frank curiosity.

It had a domed ceiling and over in one corner, there was what looked like a simple bed, made from thick, layered cloth. Mara decided it was best to ignore that, for now, as Sebastian drew her across the room.

He stopped in front of a mural covered wall. Waving his hand again, more candles were lit, illuminating the artwork.

It was exquisite.

The painting showed several scenes, depicting the lives of an outwardly human couple. They were shown surrounded by a crowd of coloured dots in groups of four; the Lifelights.

In the first scene the couple were apart, with what looked like mountains and a sea between them. In the second they were together, embracing each other, with the Lifelight dots very much in evidence. The third showed them joined by the figure of a baby, which grew into a child in the next picture. The final, fifth scene, appeared to be unfinished. It showed a woman, standing alone, a smudged area of colour off to one side of her. This may have been the beginnings of another figure, but Mara couldn't be sure. The woman in the final picture wasn't the one from the couple. *Is she the child?*

It was difficult to tell.

Sebastian was silent, his eyes moving between the paintings and Mara's face, as if waiting for something. After continuing to watch her reaction for several minutes, he slid an arm around her and turned her to face him.

"Do you like them?"

Her smile showed her appreciation better than words, "I like them very much. There's something about them… I can almost believe that I know these people." She shrugged, feeling suddenly embarrassed, "I suppose that sounds silly?"

Sebastian didn't reply. He bent his head, brushing his lips along the side of her neck. He pressed kisses in to the sensitive surface, his breath warm, as he whispered against it.

"It's not silly at all, my love. In a way you do know these people. This painting shows the story of a cycle, much like ours. This room is meant as a sanctuary, for bonded Lifelights who have found each other again. It's a place for them to remember each other."

His voice was seductive, deliberately low, so that she intuitively leant into him. She strained to hear the words clearly.

"Remember what, exactly?" She teased. Well, she wasn't that naïve. Not with that bed screaming at her from the corner of the room.

Sebastian's lips continued to graze her skin, his hands beginning a lazy exploration of her back and hips, smoothing across the material of her skirt. She could feel the heat, which was never far away, building inside her.

"It's a place to remember the touch, feel and taste of our partner, of course. That's so important, don't you think? As bonded Lifelights it's only right that we know each other… intimately."

She'd started to lose track of what they'd originally been talking about. "Hmm… sounds good."

She felt his chuckle, vibrating against the upper slope of her breasts. She really liked it when he kissed her there.

"Yes, my Mara, intimate *is* good… I want to remind you of everything that brings you pleasure… joy… ecstasy. As I think I've mentioned, I have a competitive nature. I always like to aim for ecstasy; if that's all right with you?"

"Like I'm going to argue?"

"So, you don't mind waiting, for the next question and answer session?" He asked.

She was about to reply with something rude and take matters into her own hands by giving him a push towards that bed, when she felt him stiffen against her.

And not in the way she wanted.

He groaned out loud, frustration evident, before raising his head and holding her at arm's length.

She stared at him in dawning horror, as the sound of people, moving across the cave floor outside, drifted into their room for two.

Shit.

"You're swearing again and that's 'before' you know who's out there."

He frowned as the sounds drew closer, and then called out. “You know, you could have given us a little more time. I haven’t seen her for thirty four years.”

There was the sound of laughter, from several people, hastily muffled. Then she heard a deep, male voice.

“Well *excuse* me, but I haven’t seen my Mini Mara for nineteen years. Did you really think I was going to wait around, especially with her mother bending my ear?”

Mara was sure she’d been frozen to the spot, as her eyes met Sebastian’s with disbelief.

“Is that…”

He nodded. His expression was somewhat sheepish.

“Yeah, it is. What is it about the in-laws that can strike terror into a grown man?”

CHAPTER 10

Mara flung herself into the arms of the man in front of her.

He was just as she remembered. Huge and solid. She could have been three again, wrapped in an embrace that would make a bear proud. His untamed black hair and piercing blue eyes gave him a slightly wild look.

She'd adored that about him when she was little, riding high on his massive shoulders and she adored it now, half crushed against his chest.

Tears slid down her cheeks.

It really was him. Her father, Marcus Austin

The beloved arms rocked her gently, his beard tickling her cheek as he bent his head to whisper in her ear. "Hush now, baby girl. Do you want me to shrink? Salt water can do that to a man, you know."

Raising her head for the first time, she stared up at him.

His bearded smile stretched wide, his eyes glittering with a teasing humour.

She could hardly believe it. He was here. Not dead.

"Energy doesn't die, my Mara. It converts. Take a good look at him. Look at him with Lifelight eyes." Sebastian's reassuring voice slipped into her mind.

She studied the face in front of her.

She'd been wrong, he did look different to the memory she had of him. He seemed younger, more vital.

His body had a translucent quality, mirage like. But he *felt* solid.

"Well look at you, my Mini Mara. You've grown into a beautiful woman, just as I knew you would." His voice was deep, gravelled with emotion.

Before she could reply, another voice rang through the air. This one was feminine, and just as miraculous.

"Well of course you knew that, Marcus. You've seen it happen often enough. Now put her down and let *me* see her."

Mara stared around her father's shoulder and blinked.

A tall, slender woman, the visual antithesis to Marcus, stood watching her. Long blonde hair, ruler straight, hung almost to her waist, its shining perfection eclipsed only by her eyes. Dark brown, they sparked with gold flecks. Her smile was gentle, happy, as she raised her hands. Palms upper-most, she beckoned to Mara.

"Mum." The word was softly spoken, disbelieving.

She was partially released. One of her father's thick arms still supported her as he guided her towards the woman.

Rebecca Austin's hug was tender in comparison to Marcus' but no less amazing.

Mara closed her eyes as a sigh whispered across her lips. Sebastian had tried to tell her about this. He'd said that she'd never really lost her parents, but she hadn't understood what he meant. It made her wonder about all the other things he'd told her.

Which reminded her, *"Did you say 'in-laws'? When did we get married?"*

"I may not have married you in this cycle yet, but I definitely remember doing so in earlier ones. That aside though, the fuse state is as binding as any marriage ceremony."

Mara smiled within her mother's arms.

"You're such a romantic. I'm surprised you didn't say 'we're bonded Lifelights, deal with it.'"

His silent laughter warmed her, *"Well... there are those who would put it like that."*

"Like who?"

"Your parents. This may be the twenty-first century, but Lifelights view bonding as sacred. I can guarantee you'll be getting the lecture on 'the importance of renewing your vows' at some point..."

"What did you say?" She asked, wondering at his choice of words.

There was no reply.

Worried that she'd somehow missed something important, Mara opened her eyes wide and stared over her mother's shoulder. Sebastian was nowhere to be seen. Instead, she saw a crowd, gathered behind them. There were too many figures to count. They were spread out through the cavern, every face turned towards them. The sound of whispered conversation filled the air.

She saw children in amongst the adults. All boys.

That's strange.

She tried to remember everything Sebastian had told her. He'd said something about the women getting their gifts when they turned twenty two... *is* that *why there aren't any little girls here?*

Mara felt her mother move away. She now faced the assembled Lifelights, flanked by her parents. Her nerves began to rise, even as she felt Sebastian's presence behind her. She didn't like not being able to see him. *"Stay with me, please."*

"Don't worry; I'm here, my Mara."

Relief flooded through her at his answer, his deep voice easily audible throughout the cavern.

Beside her, Marcus' body filled with tension. He turned his head, staring over hers. Looking up she saw that his eyes had narrowed as they focused on Sebastian.

"So, you're here once more, Mr. Oran." His resonant voice rumbled through the air of the cave. The candle flames flickered, as if in reaction to the power layered within it. "Are you determined to take our daughter from us then, when we've only just found her again?"

Mara stiffened. It wasn't difficult to hear the challenge in her father's voice. Rebecca hugged her closer, her hands rubbing her back in soothing strokes.

For a moment there was silence.

But she was having none of it.

Looking at her parents and then Sebastian, *my lover,* she felt the shift inside her and knew what she had to do. She pulled away from Rebecca and Marcus, stepping back.

Then she reached out to the person who'd come to mean so much to her, *in such a short space of time.*

"You think three billion years is a short space of time?"

"Shut up, Sebastian. I'm still having trouble with that particular concept."

"Your family love you; don't worry, I'm used to this, my love."

"Well I'm not. Now take my hand and let me handle this."

Sebastian sighed, *"Very well, my Mara, but can I just say something?"*

"What?"

"I think I could grow to love your dominant side."

There was a definite leer to the words.

"Sebastian..."

As soon as she felt his hand wrap around hers, before she even realised she was doing it, she sent him a wave of love and reassurance. It was the most complicated thing she'd attempted, so far. Emotion soared outwards, from her mind into his, rippling between them in a heated tide.

At the same time, she looked towards the assemble Lifelights.

Her chin went up. She *wouldn't* be intimidated. Sebastian's fingers tightened around her hand. His support gave her the strength she needed.

"Be careful what you say, Dad. I wouldn't be here if it weren't for Sebastian. I won't stay if he leaves."

Mara's voice had changed. She sounded stronger, even to her own ears. For too many years she'd allowed herself to be a captive of her past. She'd mourned the deaths of her parents and grandparents. She'd relied heavily on the Lifelights and Jennie, for company and to give her life purpose. There was no way she was going back to that.

Sebastian had searched for her, claimed her. He'd shown her some of their long history together. She wanted more of the same. The strength of their connection was addictive.

Total silence reigned as Marcus stared at her, his eyes steady on her for several long moments. Mara didn't break eye contact with him. She allowed herself to be drawn in to Sebastian's side, his arm around her waist, firm and possessive. It seemed almost a lifetime ago that she'd worried about him taking over her life. Now she relished the feeling of power, that each of them had over the other.

The whispering became more urgent, spreading across the cave, as the Lifelights began to turn to each other. They appeared unsure what to do.

Marcus Austin, however, was now staring at his daughter with something very close to amusement on his face. He glanced down at his wife and Rebecca rolled her eyes, her mouth curving into a small smile, "*Why* do we have to have this *every* time?"

Marcus shrugged, "I have no idea what you're talking about, Rebecca."

"Hmm, I just bet you don't. What I'm *talking* about, is this silly posturing you and Sebastian insist on. How many cycles have these two been together?

"Will you for once just tell Mara that you love her, that you want nothing more than her happiness and that you would be proud to welcome Sebastian to our branch of the family?"

Marcus made a feeble attempt at protest. "Proud? I think not; that would be going too far. I would hate it if our daughter's partner were to get complacent about his position."

Rebecca frowned up at her husband. "Like that's ever going to happen. You really are too bad. Why can't you admit that you like having him around?"

Marcus sounded like he was choking, but Rebecca ignored him. Instead she turned towards Mara and Sebastian. "I'm very pleased that you've found each other again. Please, come and meet your brothers and sisters, Mara."

"Brothers and sisters?"

The shock she felt when Rebecca indicated the crowd of Lifelights in front of them, was quickly overtaken by the sensation of amusement, both heard and felt, as it passed from Sebastian to her.

"It's a figure of speech, my love. These are not actually your brothers and sisters. They are your fellow Lifelights and, as such, your family. Slioch is one of our spiritual homes. The people here are those who responded to the call. They've come from all over the

world to greet you and welcome you back 'into the fold', as it were."

"There are more Lifelights?" Mara had assumed that this was it.

Sebastian chuckled, burying his face in her hair. She could feel him shaking with suppressed mirth, *"Oh yes, my love, there are definitely more Lifelights. You wouldn't believe how many. In this cycle, I belong to the American branch of the 'family' and after them; my loyalty is with my mother's Italian relatives."*

"You see right there, I lose It." She confessed, staring round at the expectant faces in front of them, *"The cycles are the most confusing part of all this. I don't understand them. I don't understand how I could have had parents and grandparents or how you can appear twelve years older than me, when we're the same age. It doesn't make sense."*

"Ah, but it makes perfect sense. You said the crucial word, 'appear'. That's all our human hidden state is, an illusion."

Sebastian nuzzled her hair, his arm pulling her closer. His fingers splayed wide, pressing against her waist. *"You will never be as old as I, to a casual human observer, but we will forever be old souls. I for one am thankful that we've been together for so long. There are still Lifelights in the world who haven't bonded as we have, haven't found the Lifelight meant for them. The eternity that is a Lifelight's existence would be a cold and lonely place without you, my love."*

As Sebastian's words whispered across her mind, Mara felt as if she were melting. No one had ever said anything like that to her before *in this lifetime*.

Their silent conversation was interrupted by Marcus, as he threw up his hands and gave a disgruntled snort, "Oh for pity's sake, just look at them Rebecca! I swear they get more besotted with every cycle!" He sounded thoroughly exasperated as he stared at his daughter and 'son-in-law'.

"That is as it should be. Would you want it any other way?" Rebecca asked, rubbing her hand up and down her husband's arm.

Marcus shrugged, although he still managed to glare at Sebastian. "I suppose not. It's just that I *was* hoping for some time alone with our daughter before she's spirited away… to America of all places!"

Mara had to laugh at that, she couldn't help it. "You can stop trying to get my sympathy vote *Daddy.* I've found out enough, about what I am, to know that a trip to America would take all of three seconds. That's hardly an unreasonable amount of travelling time, especially if it's to see family."

"But you're my daughter…" Marcus began.

She jumped at the opening, "Yes. About that, how *can* you be my father? I've tried to understand, but the whole family thing has me confused."

It was Rebecca who answered her. "We are your parents in *this* cycle, Mara, just as we have had the honour of being your parents in other cycles. It isn't always that way though.

"Sometimes you are born to others."

CHAPTER 11

"I am?" Shock pitched Mara's voice higher than usual.

Rebecca nodded, before taking her hand and pulling her away from Sebastian. She steered her across the cavern.

The assembled Lifelights parted without a sound, clearing a path to one of the mural covered walls.

Standing before it, her arm linked through her mother's, Mara stared up at the intricate paintings.

"This is our history." Rebecca said, her arm sweeping out to encompass everything in front of them, "Look carefully, Mara. You can see the moment of our birth, an explosion of power at a time of great upheaval. You can see the early years, when our natural form was all we knew and our intellect was in its infancy. That period lasted a *long* time." She pointed further along the wall, to a picture that was particularly well lit. "And there, you see the moment when we mastered the mutation of matter. We can become anything living, animal or plant, that relies on energy for its survival. Not that we do. We prefer to keep things simple.

"The moment you see illustrated here was also the point that, as a species, we developed a conscience and moral code. We realised that our powers needed to be held in check, so that other life would also have a chance to flourish."

Mara was astonished. The Lifelights could easily have altered the development of so many species. "Why did we think that was so important?" She asked.

Rebecca shrugged. "One reason only. We fell in love with the human race. See? The paintings give a hint of how fascinated we were with them. They were the first creatures we could interact and communicate with. It didn't take long for us to devise a plan that would allow us to co-exist with them and watch them develop."

"The cycles..." Mara breathed. Her gaze roamed across the surface of the wall as she tried her best to make sense of what she was seeing there.

"Yes." Rebecca replied, "The cycles. We devised a way of creating what were essentially cadavers, lifeless bodies that had the ability to age as a human would. Then we experimented. We found that we could create any number of them, but without that spark of life, they were useless to us.

"Finally we managed to form bodies 'around' our natural form. We then modified them, so that they responded to our energy. This allowed us to manipulate them, giving the appearance of life. We became so adept at this that soon the difference between us and humans was undetectable. We could do anything with our new bodies; even change between forms. The only thing our illusion of humanity couldn't do was survive the fuse state. After each fuse, even now, we have to create a new body. It's an automatic process."

Mara was silent as she allowed that to sink in, "You mean the body I have now isn't the same one I had yesterday?"

Laughter greeted her question, rippling through the gathered Lifelights.

"Way to go, my love, you've just confirmed what we've been up to..."

Mara's cheeks burned. *"You could have told me about this before. I have a body that's replaced after each fuse state? Come on, Sebastian, that idea has so much potential! Instant weight loss and zero cellulite spring to mind..."*

Sebastian laughed, *"It's never a good idea to create too many changes. Humans tend to notice. That brings its own set of problems."*

Still cringing slightly at the thought of her faux-pas, Mara turned to look at her mother. "Is that where the idea of immortals comes from? There are so many human myths about species that live forever. Does that stem from their interaction with us?"

Rebecca frowned, considering the question for a moment, "Yes, I'd say that's possible. We weren't as careful in the beginning as we are now. Although the cadavers aged, from birth to adulthood and into old age, we weren't adept at synchronising that aging process with the humans around us. It took many years to perfect the cycles, but eventually we came up with the version we use now. It seems to work well for us, apart from the glitch regarding our females."

"Glitch?"

Marcus, who'd been very quiet so far, came to stand at Mara's side. He too stared at the murals. He touched her arm, drawing her attention to one that showed something very similar to the last painting she'd looked at in the small chamber. It showed the figure of an apparently human woman with a blurred patch of colour beside her.

"That is a representation of the 'glitch' Rebecca is telling you about. The human families we create are an illusion. We create phantom pregnancies, with apparently viable foetuses that grow inside their mothers just as a human baby would. But it's all show. The cadaver is nothing more than an empty shell up until the moment of its 'birth'. That's when the next Lifelight due to be born enters the body and begins the human part of the cycle. It it's a boy, then the Lifelight in question loses none of his knowledge and understands exactly what he is from birth onwards. However, for some reason, our women…" he trailed off, as if at a loss how to explain further.

"Lose everything." Mara finished for him.

"Yes, and we have no idea why. They lose all memory and self-awareness as a Lifelight until about their twenty-second birthday. Then something changes, their powers and memories begin to return and they are thrown into a race for their lives. Their human life, that is. If they don't meet their bonded partner, can't make the first change for whatever reason, then they die; ripped apart by the very energy that drives us. Luckily, that doesn't happen often."

Marcus looked down at Mara, whose cheeks were still red with embarrassment, "In that regard, I can't thank Sebastian enough. Without him you couldn't have made the change. Once Lifelights become bonded, the female *needs* the energy spike that the male creates with her. It kick-starts the change, gives her back her knowledge and talents."

Okay, so now my 'Dad' is saying he's okay with me having sex with Sebastian. Mara closed her eyes. *Could this get any more embarrassing?*

"I'd say you're over the worst of it." Sebastian commented, coming up behind her to wrap his arms around her waist.

"My head hurts." Mara confessed out loud.

"I'm not surprised. I think you've learned enough for now. Your mother has adequately covered the cycle basics. The important fact is we are born into bodies that appear to age and then die. Then we wait in our natural state for the humans we knew to forget us or even pass away, before we are re-born into another body. Re-birth is done by strict rotation, so that bonded Lifelights are always born within the same generation."

"But not necessarily to the same parents?"

"No."

Sebastian turned her away from the murals and spoke directly to her parents. "Mara's on the point of overload. Maybe it's time to introduce her to the rest of the family, as you suggested earlier, Rebecca."

Smiling in gratitude Mara allowed herself to be pulled forward by the three of them, conscious of their protective presence beside her.

The rest of the Lifelights began to move forward, murmuring greetings to her, expressing their pleasure that she was back in Slioch.

It was easy to tell the difference between the more solid figures, Lifelights who were in their human forms and the subtle shimmer of those between bodies.

A group of twelve 'between bodies' Lifelights approached them. Mara looked at them, puzzled. They seemed nervous.

At the same time, every face within the group gave her a feeling of peace, but it was the faces of the couple at the head of the group that gave her the strongest feeling – of belonging.

Her eyes widened with shocked recognition.

Their faces may look young and beautiful now, but their features were embedded in her memory for all time.

Without a word they held out their arms and Mara flew into them.

Her grandfather smiled down at her, "Hello again, darling girl." He whispered, "Missed us?" Mara promptly burst into tears. His voice was so dear to her; she would have known it anywhere.

Looking over her grandparents' shoulders, she saw the smiling faces of the others in the group and realised who they were.

"You're *my* Lifelights, aren't you?" She whispered, "The ones who came to me when I was a little girl."

The faces continued to smile as heads nodded. Mara felt her grandmother's grip tighten on her. "You see, little one, there was no way that we would ever abandon you. The car crash was serious; no human could have survived it. Marcus and Rebecca had no choice but to take on their natural form and abandon their human bodies. They'd grown so fond of you. It was a difficult decision for them. The temptation to reveal their presence to you, comfort you and reassure you that the crash had not really killed them was almost overwhelming.

"Can you imagine trying to explain *that* to a three year old, who couldn't remember a thing about what she really was? In the end, they could only bring themselves to visit you at night, when you were sleeping and unaware, but their need to protect you was still strong.

"When Rebecca called out to our family for help, these are the Lifelights who answered her."

Tears ran down Mara's cheeks as she stared at the faces around her. "How can I thank you?" She whispered.

In answer *her* Lifelights gathered closer. They reached out to touch her. Then a couple pushed forward. The woman was petite; the man beside her dwarfed her tiny frame. "We are your family. There is no need to thank any of us. We two, however, would ask for your forgiveness."

Mara brushed at her tears. "My forgiveness, for what?" She asked.

The couple looked uncomfortable; eventually the man spoke, "For being the first to leave you. Our only excuse is that we were spreading the word to your immediate family. We went to your parents; let them know that you had started to come into your powers. We told them that Sebastian had arrived to claim you."

Sebastian took that as his cue to wrap both arms around her from behind. He pulled her into him.

At the same time she heard her father 'cough'. "Speaking of Sebastian 'claiming' Mara, don't you think it's about time we got on with finishing that?"

Mara could feel her eyebrows knitting together. She turned her head to look at her parents, "What do you mean?" She asked.

Marcus beamed at her, "Why, the renewal of your marriage vows, of course!"

"Guess that was your 'you're bonded Lifelights, deal with it' moment?" Mara asked, leaning back into Sebastian.

Sebastian tightened his grip on her and bent to nuzzle her hair, something he seemed to enjoy doing, "*I also think that's your father's way of saying he's 'okay' with us, my darling. So...*

"Will you marry me, Mara?"

Every previously tensed muscle relaxed, as happiness coursed through her. Turning in Sebastian's arms, she stared up at him, sending him all the love and happiness she was feeling, directly into his mind. Her heart beat faster as she felt his answering emotion, flooding her mind. There was love, happiness and an underlying hunger.

"Yes." She replied simply.

Sebastian's head lowered as he kissed her soundly, whilst Marcus merely grunted, "I should think so too!"

Giving herself up to Sebastian's kiss, Mara couldn't help smiling inside. Grouch that her father appeared to be, it was obvious that he loved her. The knowledge warmed her.

Suddenly Sebastian's mouth left hers.

Slightly stunned, Mara opened her eyes. He'd swung his head round, his eyes narrowed, as if searching for something. He pulled her to his side, just as the figure of a woman appeared.

She stood directly in front of them.

Tall, slim and gorgeous, her long strawberry blonde hair was swept up, in an elegant chignon. The style successfully displayed an enviably long neck and smooth, blemish free skin. Her clothes consisted of a professional looking, but nonetheless flattering, navy blue skirt suit with a white blouse beneath and impossibly high heels, in the same navy colour as the suit. Her body appeared solid, which meant that she was currently in the human part of the cycle and Mara would have guessed that her age was somewhere between late thirties to early forties.

"Alexa," Sebastian said, immediately identifying the woman, but Mara's attention was too focused on what the woman was carrying to pay much attention. *What's she doing with my handbag?*

"I'm sorry for intruding, Sebastian, but this couldn't wait." Alexa held out the bag towards Mara. "I was collecting the car to take it back to our office, when I noticed this and realised you needed it."

"Why would you think that?" Mara asked.

Alexa smiled, "Because *my* gift is the energy of communication - microwaves, and I could tell that this was about to start..." She trailed off and once again offered the bag to Mara, just as the sound of her favourite rock music filled the air, "Ringing." She finished.

Wondering briefly how she was getting a signal, in the middle of a cave, Mara hastily dug out her mobile phone.

It must be a 'Lifelight thing' she decided.

As she answered the phone, a feeling of unease swept through her, "Hello?"

Who could be ringing me?

"Mara?" the voice that answered sounded strained.

Jennie.

"Oh, Mara, thank goodness you picked up!" Strain had turned in to panic, "Look, I'm sorry to bother you, but I think I'm in trouble. I've just had a visit from two men, from the café's electricity supplier."

Stunned, Mara's voice came out barely above a whisper, "Your electricity supplier?"

Sebastian's eyes narrowed as he openly eavesdropped.

"I don't understand, Jennie. What has that got to do with me?"

Her friend let out a gusty sigh, "I really wish I knew, Mara. All they'd say was that they're also investigating some discrepancies in *your* energy usage. They mentioned something about a recent power spike at the cottage. Then they told me that they have concerns about the amount of power we were using at the café…" Jennie's voice trailed off.

"Do they think the café's using more power than it should?" Mara asked, trying to keep her voice calm.

"No!" Jennie all but wailed, "That's the horrible part about this! They said that we weren't using *enough* energy for a business like this. They're accusing me of defrauding them and they threatened me with court action! Unless…" Jennie's voice gave out on her totally this time.

"Unless what, Jennie?" Mara coaxed. She heard her friend take a deep, steadying breath before she answered.

"Unless you come back and speak to them; they said that they thought you were the person responsible for the strange readings, but that they wouldn't hesitate to name me as a co-conspirator to fraud if you refused to cooperate with them.

"Mara, I could lose my business over this! I could go to jail! Please, I know you wouldn't do anything illegal, but if you could just come back and explain everything, I know we can sort this mess out!"

Mara was trembling now. Her frightened eyes locked with Sebastian's swirling silver gaze. "Don't you worry, Jennie; of course I'll come back. Tell the electricity company I'm on my way."

After saying her goodbyes, she closed her phone with a snap and looked at Sebastian.

His expression was thunderous.

It didn't take a genius to realise that this was bad; *very* bad.

CHAPTER 12

Marcus had growling down to a fine art.

"What do you mean, 'the wedding's off'?"

Mara winced as his voice bounced off the cavern walls, "Calm down, Dad. Maybe 'off' was the wrong word to use. Postponed would be more accurate."

The distinction didn't seem to help.

"Oh come on, you don't seriously expect me to hang around here when Jennie is in trouble do you?"

Sebastian, standing beside her, suddenly looked down. Glancing across at him, Mara saw his mouth twitch and his head give a tiny shake, as though he couldn't quite believe she was arguing with her Dad.

After a few moments of speechlessness, Marcus found his voice. He used it to good effect. "You are my daughter, Mara, and under the protection of not only your mother and I, but also the British Lifelights. It will probably come as no surprise, but I've always considered Sebastian to be a bad influence on you. This though, is going too far. I'll be damned if I'll let the two of you go gallivanting round the country *without* renewing your vows!"

By the time Marcus had reached the end of his tirade, his voice had risen significantly, growling left far behind in favour of roaring.

"Well, you'd better prepare to be damned then, because I am *not* getting married again until this mess is sorted out!" Mara was surprised to find that her own voice rivalled her father's when it came to volume.

Looking more than a little uncomfortable, Rebecca stepped between her husband and daughter. She took one of both Mara's and Marcus' hands as she did so, linking them. Her eyes were imploring, "Would the two of you *please* stop arguing? You both have appalling tempers, when you really should know better. Yelling at each other isn't going to solve anything."

Mara looked apologetically at her mother but refused to back down where her father was concerned. "He started it." She pointed out, anger still at the forefront of her mind.

Rebecca rolled her eyes. It was a move that looked more practiced than it should, but it was the soft chuckle that escaped from Sebastian that finally defused the situation. He was still studying the cavern floor and proving annoyingly difficult to read.

"If you don't calm down, Mara, you may not get the chance to sort out Jennie's problem."

"Why not?" She asked.

Sebastian stopped studying the floor and looked up. He stared directly at her, the silver in his eyes swirling brightly, his expression suddenly hungry, *"Because, my darling, I'll have carried you off to have my wicked way with you. Have I never told you? You are truly beautiful when you get angry. Magnificent; and that makes me want you – now."*

Mara swallowed, unable to stop the instant rush of heat that flooded her mind and body. *"I wouldn't go quietly, Sebastian."* Even in her mind, she could hear the breathless quality of her voice.

Sebastian shrugged, pulling her away from her parents and cradling her close to his aroused body. *"Perhaps not, but by the time I took you you'd want me just as badly and neither of us would be thinking of anything else; certainly not Jennie."*

"You reckon?"

"Do you want to put it to the test, my Mara, or are you and your father going to come to an agreement? Magnificent as you are, your mother is getting upset."

She sagged at that, resting her forehead against his chest for a moment before she turned to face her parents.

"Look, I'm not doing any of this to spite you. I just want to get this problem sorted out before I do anything else. Jennie has been good to me and I'm not going to abandon her now. It's my fault she's in this situation and I want to fix it for her. Is that wrong of me?"

There was complete silence in the cave. The rest of the Lifelights were so still, they could have been statues. Marcus stared at Mara, before turning towards Rebecca, his eyes wary and his head slightly tilted, as if he were listening to something. Mara wondered if her mother was giving him telepathic 'hell'.

He rubbed his hand across his forehead, holding it there for a moment, as if deep in thought. Then, finally, he turned back to them, pulling Rebecca against his side as he did so, his embrace one of comfort.

Marcus' deep voice rumbled through the cave once again, quiet now, but no less powerful. "No, it isn't wrong, Mara, but please try to understand; it's difficult for us let you go. This situation could be extremely dangerous for all of us. I understand your reasons for wanting to help Jennie but, before you go, I would ask something of you."

After a slight hesitation, Mara nodded.

Marcus visibly relaxed. "I want you to promise me that you won't hesitate to contact us if this meeting, between you and the electricity company, goes badly. I don't care whether it's the British Lifelights, those

Sebastian knows or all of us, but I want your word that you won't try to handle things on your own. The Lifelights are your family and, as such, we demand the right to protect you. Do you agree?"

Marcus' face was solemn as he waited for Mara's reply.

The thought that there were potentially dozens of Lifelights wanting to help her, was almost too much for Mara. She struggled to find her voice, ever aware of Sebastian by her side. Love and understanding flooded into her mind, directly from his.

A few short days ago she'd been almost alone, not realising who she was or what the Lifelights were. Now she had more family than she could have dreamed of and a partner who had, if she believed him, been with her for billions of years. The feeling of belonging had always been something that was missing from her life. Now, she had it all.

Her voice was husky with emotion when she finally replied, "I agree, and I understand. Thank you for being there for me."

Marcus looked as though he too was struggling to contain his emotions. Stepping forward, with Rebecca at his side, he kissed Mara on the forehead. Then he turned to Sebastian.

Without hesitation Sebastian clasped and shook the proffered hand, "Don't worry, either of you, I'll take good care of her. You can rest assured that *I* will not hesitate to call on the help of others, should the need arise."

Tension evaporated. One step forward and they were hugging each other; Mara, Sebastian, Rebecca and Marcus, whilst the rest of the Lifelights moved to encircle them.

All except Alexa; she waited patiently by the entrance to the cave, her beautiful face unreadable as she watched them. Eventually though, her voice broke through the feeling of happiness that was starting to fill the cave.

"We need to leave. The electricity company will be expecting Mara and unless you want to create more suspicion, the two of you will not be able to travel with our usual speed. I suggest you take the car and set off immediately."

She was right, of course, but Mara could have cried. The thought of leaving her family, so soon after they had discovered each other again, wasn't one she wanted to deal with. Forcing herself to appear calm, she gave her parents and grandparents one last hug. Then she turned towards Sebastian, her resolve not to show emotion wavering. She saw the understanding in his eyes, his pride in her swirling through her mind.

She took comfort from the arms that he slid around her waist. Laying her head against his shoulder, she closed her eyes. His voice soothed her, "*That's it, my love, trust me. We will deal with this threat to Jennie and then we will give your parents what they wish for – our marriage for this cycle.*"

He turned briefly to face the Lifelights. "We will return soon," he stated, simply, before opening his mind to Mara's and allowing her to use his detailed memories. In an instant, they'd left Slioch behind and were standing by the side of the car.

Alexa was already there, awaiting instructions. Barely glancing at her, Sebastian helped Mara into the car, before walking around to the driver's side. It was only then that he spoke to Alexa. His voice was grave.

"I want you to go to Jennie. She's spoken with you before so should accept your presence. Introduce yourself properly and explain that I've sent you to be with her until we can be there ourselves. Try to get as much information as you can about the people who visited her and find out exactly what they said to her. We need to know who we're dealing with.

"I want to be certain that the company is a purely British concern and not linked to any of the larger energy companies from America, Russia, China or the Middle East. If they are, we'll need to know the details of the parent company – the names of the chief executive, the directors and any major shareholders, together with the location of the head office."

Alexa nodded, her face serious, "I'll see to it. All the information will be waiting for you on your arrival back at The Tea Cosy," she paused, before quietly adding, "Look after yourselves."

As soon as she'd finished speaking she disappeared from sight, leaving Sebastian to climb into the car beside Mara.

They were speeding back towards England, and Jennie, within the minute.

* * * *

They'd been driving for about an hour, in total silence, when Mara decided she couldn't stand it any longer. Despite the waves of reassurance that Sebastian was constantly sending her, her nerves were more on edge with each passing mile.

Questions crowded into her mind, demanding answers. Was Jennie all right? Were the people from the electricity company simply following up on a suspected fraud case or was there something more sinister going on? What if she, Mara, messed up during the interview with these people and made things worse? What would happen to the Lifelights, to her and Sebastian, if she couldn't keep her mouth shut?

"You worry too much." Sebastian whispered quietly. He reached out, his fingers gentle as they covered her hands, where they lay clasped together in her lap.

Looking up at him, she felt a tingle of awareness shoot through her. She shook her head in wonder. How was it that, even as worried and stressed as she felt now, one look at him and her body responded like paper to a flame? It didn't seem right somehow.

"Oh, it's right, my love. We Lifelights are a highly responsive species. On our own, we are only a shadow of our true potential but when we find our partner, bond and fuse, we become whole. Our emotional and physical needs are doubled, feeding off those of our partner. What you're feeling now is not disloyal to Jennie. You could easily have stayed in Scotland, but that never occurred to you.

"Do not confuse your strong connection to me with a lack of connection to others. You're powerful, Mara, a Lifelight. Accept your nature. What you are, what we share, doesn't make you less of a friend to Jennie.

"In the end, it may be the one thing that allows you to save her."

She understood what he was telling her, sort of, but worry for her friend was still a shadow in her mind, as was the guilt, "It might be true that I have the potential to save Jennie, but it's also true that it's her connection to me that caused her problems in the first place. Not only that, I'm frightened about making trouble for the Lifelights. What if, by talking to me, the electricity company confirms that I'm responsible for the unusual power readings at the cottage and café? What if someone higher up in the energy industry is behind this situation and I mess up, giving away what I am?"

She could feel Sebastian's frustration, his need to protect her by whatever means he could. His emotions swept through her and she began to understand.

Sebastian was with her, through thick and thin, and he would help her all he could. He mentally bombarded her with the intensity of his feelings, demanded that she listen to him, trust him, at the deepest level possible. She wasn't on her own any more. They'd fused. Their minds, souls and bodies had blended, into a seamless whole.

As she allowed this knowledge to take root in her mind, she sensed his body begin to relax beside her. Her own muscles followed his lead, her hands turning so that they could hold on to him, their fingers twining together.

It was another turning point.

They continued on in this way for another hour or so, their minds linked and emotions rippling unhindered between them. There was no need for verbal conversation.

Eventually her mind began to wander, her thoughts turning to the Lifelights, miles away in Slioch, to Alexa and the American and Italian Lifelights that Sebastian had mentioned.

"Tell me about your family. Is Alexa related to you?"

"Yes, but only in the same way that you are related to the British Lifelights. I was born into the American branch of the Lifelight family, a family which is global. As I've said, the cycles are done in strict rotation when it comes to bonded pairs, so that they stay within a generation, but other than that…" he paused, "I'm not sure how to explain it, other than to say that the cycles are fairly 'loose' when it comes to other details. Any one of us can be dropped somewhere new, although our longevity means that most countries have been covered by now."

"So… in the next cycle I could be the one born in Italy and you the one born in England?" She asked, "I wonder why that is?"

"I don't think there's a single Lifelight who knows the answer to that. The best that we've been able to come up with is, whatever triggered our birth in the first place is also the trigger behind our decision to mimic humans and the driving force behind our development. Who knows, perhaps energy has an instinct for survival that pushes it/us to learn everything we can about the environment we're born into? That would explain the shift in Lifelight population between different countries. It allows every Lifelight to learn about human society, wherever they find themselves."

"It's a possibility," Mara agreed. Minutes passed as she turned the idea over in her mind.

The countryside flashed past her window, not nearly quick enough for her liking. She supposed a speeding ticket would be a disaster though. The last thing they needed was a Police record.

"Actually, that would be the least of our worries. An accident, on such a public road, would be more of a problem."

"Why? Other than the obvious of course - I'd hate you to dent this beauty."

Sebastian laughed, "I think you have your priorities wrong, my Mara. The reason that an accident would be a problem is the possible need for medical attention."

"But… I thought we could heal ourselves? You did that cool trick with my finger and we can create new bodies, so what problem would a few broken bones cause us?"

"None, if we could persuade those around us not to send us to the hospital. Unfortunately, if we couldn't, we'd probably have to make our injuries fatal… to preserve our secret."

"Like my parents did?" She asked.

"Exactly; either that or we allow ourselves to be treated but make sure that no blood samples etcetera are taken."

Mara didn't understand the reasons for that. "But I thought that our bodies were perfect copies?"

"They are perfect illusions. When we cut ourselves, we appear to bleed, but it's not real blood. When we get a headache, it's not physiological, it's psychological. We appear to have an inbuilt instinct for when to display a human trait or weakness.

"Anyone possessing a Lifelight 'blood' sample would quickly find themselves with a mystery on their hands, unless they were treating a Chemical Lifelight."

That last sentence, delivered casually, shocked Mara. "Whoa! Hang on a minute… a Chemical Lifelight? What's one of those and why are *they* different when it comes to seeing a doctor?"

For some reason, Sebastian looked ashamed. "I'm sorry, I shouldn't have mentioned that. You have enough to understand without me adding more."

She folded her arms. *"Spit it out, Sebastian."*

"I can't. I'm sorry, but that's a part of our history that you don't need to know right now. It's complicated. I don't even know where to start on the subject, without it reflecting badly on our species. Please, let it go."

"Okay. I'll let it go, for now, but that doesn't mean that I'm never going to ask you about it. When I do, I want answers."

"Fair enough," he agreed.

She didn't miss the whisper of relief that briefly touched his mind, or the fact that all thoughts about the Chemical Lifelights quickly disappeared.

CHAPTER 13

Mara continued to stare out at the passing scenery, her thoughts drifting. *It's strange that Lifelights seem to be closer if they share a talent, rather than a relationship. Not sure if I'll ever get used to that. I'm too used to being around humans, watching the people who come to the café, where the tie between blood relatives is stronger than a friendship formed through a common interest.*

Beside her, Sebastian barked out a laugh. She turned to look at him, raising one eyebrow. "Were you eavesdropping again?" She asked.

He didn't even have the grace to look embarrassed. "Yeah, it's sort of addictive. I love the way your mind works."

"I'm not sure that's a compliment when you find my thoughts so amusing." She pointed out.

Sebastian grinned at her, "Only you would compare the manipulation of electricity to a 'common interest'. Are you sure about what you were thinking though? Surely it's a common interest that pulls a lot of human couples together? Theirs is not a blood tie but it can be just as strong, if not stronger, than any family ties."

Mara thought about that for a minute or two. "I suppose you have a point, although I'd argue that it's far more than a common interest that holds human couples together. There's also physical attraction."

Sebastian looked smug, "There you are then, and it's not so different to us. You and I definitely have a strong attraction to each other both mentally, through the way we communicate, and physically." His voice dropped lower on the final word, his eyes beginning to swirl with silver as he looked across at her.

Mara shoved at the hand that had crept onto her lap, caressing her. Her laughter left her no option but to switch communication methods, *"Behave yourself, Sebastian! We have to keep focused. Concentrate. How am I going to deal with this interview?"*

"All you have to do is plead ignorant. If you stick to that story, then it's up to them to prove otherwise. And believe me, there'll be plenty of evidence that proves your innocence. *I'll* make sure of that."

"What if the company is linked to something bigger?"

"We'll cross that bridge if we come to it. It's pointless second-guessing our game plan until we have whatever information Alexa uncovers." His voice was calm, steadying her nerves.

She decided to change the subject.

"About Alexa, it was good of her to come all this way to help us. After all, the poor woman only thought she was picking up a car! Why was she doing that by the way? Couldn't someone else do it, from your office here?"

Sebastian smiled, "No, because there are no Lifelights employed in the English offices and only a Lifelight can drive this car. With Alexa the performance wouldn't have been great, but at least it would have moved!"

Mara thought about that. At last she figured it out, and found herself smiling too.

"That separate power source you told me about; it's us isn't it? I don't believe this; I've been reduced to being fuel for a car! And before you ask, no, I don't care how impressive it is!" She tried to make her voice fierce, which was difficult, with a huge smile plastered across her face.

Sebastian's voice dipped low, "You think this car is merely impressive? I'd have described it as sexy myself, which makes it entirely appropriate that you should be powering it."

Mara shook her head, "You talk a load of rubbish sometimes Sebastian Oran; you do know that, don't you? I suppose Alexa would struggle to power this car because her 'talent' is for microwaves, not electricity? I bet she was relieved when she didn't have to drive it back to the office after all, not to mention her partner. In fact, come to think of it, I'm rather impressed she turned up at all. I know how over-protective you can get with me, so I'm pleasantly surprised that her partner let her come here by herself. I'm assuming she does have a partner, back in America?" Mara knew she was prattling, but couldn't seem to help it. Sebastian tended to have that effect on her.

It wasn't until he went suddenly still and quiet that she managed to stop.

He was looking distracted.

She frowned, wondering what she'd said, but a second later she relaxed again as he began to speak, "Actually, yes, Alexa does have a partner in America, her husband Ross; she also has a daughter, Rosalyn."

Her mouth fell open slightly with this revelation. "Wow, I'm *really* impressed then. I wonder if Ross knows *all* that's going on though. I can't see you being that understanding, if it was me skipping between continents. Especially if it had the potential to turn dangerous and we had a child." She stopped abruptly, blushing scarlet as she realised what she'd said.

Turning to the window, she studiously avoided looking at him.

He'd gone quiet again, the silence between them stretching out. She couldn't even get an idea about his thoughts. He seemed to be quite adept at blocking her when he wanted to. Or maybe she just needed more practice?

She stiffened, as he slowed the car, pulling it over to the road side.

Am I in trouble? She wondered. Then she jumped, as his hands took hold of her shoulders.

The air inside the car seemed to crystallise with tension.

She felt herself being turned, until she had no choice but look at him.

What she saw there instantly had her heart pounding against her chest, its pace frenetic. She became aware of every pulse point. Her breath rushing between her parted lips, as it attempted to keep up with her heart's thunderous, slightly erratic rhythm.

In a bid to regain control, she drew in a sharp breath. She'd never seen his eyes look so intense. Silver blazed at her and everything within her responded instantly. Waves of emotion poured out of her, to collide with the thick blanket of feeling that suddenly and relentlessly pushed out from Sebastian's mind. It ensnared her, wrapped itself around her conscious thoughts. Until emotion was all there was.

Her eyes widened, as she recognised that she was powerless. She couldn't fight this, even if she wanted to. Sensation rushed through her; love, yes, but also a deep longing and a ruthless desire that charged ahead of it all.

Whatever he needed her to understand, to him, it was more important than anything else that had gone before.

"When we have children of our own, the next cycle of Lifelights, you will have to promise me something." His voice was thick, a muted trickle of sound, "You must promise me that you will be strong, and that you will fight to keep me in check. I do not think you will have a life otherwise; my instincts will be to lock you away, all of you, somewhere safe where nothing ugly or dangerous could ever touch you.

"I love you, my Mara, but I am well aware of my shortfalls. I have a tendency to be domineering, when it comes to your welfare. I also know that I'm likely to get worse, when we have young ones to care for; especially if we're blessed with a female Lifelight."

Mara relaxed. Slowly she raised her hand to gently trace down the side of his beloved face, so close to her own. "Now who's worrying over nothing? I know you better than you think, Sebastian.

"I have a confession. My memories of our lives together are starting to return. I'm beginning to remember so many things… including our fights. They've always been a passionate and important part of our relationship, as has 'making up'. We'll have to learn from each other, that's what relationships are all about... However long they last."

The pupils in Sebastian's eyes expanded, the irises shining, liquid silver, showing her everything she needed to know. Looking into his eyes was like looking into his soul. Once she saw past the dazzling display, every dark corner of his mind, every fear, every hope for the future, was there. It was highlighted, with nothing hidden.

There was so much love for her.

With a soft moan of acceptance, she pushed herself

forward. She tilted back her head, in total surrender of what he was. What they both were.

Sebastian responded immediately, pinning her lips beneath his. Their kiss was fiercely heated, as if they were branding each other. A bone deep ache rose up inside them, shared through their link. It morphed into a burning need that swept through their minds and bodies; pure energy.

Electricity was everywhere, snapping its way through them, escaping where it could. It seared their skin until it threatened to melt the thin barrier that dared to separate them. It caressed, filled and possessed them.

In a single life-defining second she felt pleasure, bordering on pain. It travelled through her mind, forced open doors that had been closed for years. Gone was the gradual return of memories, instead, everything that she'd thought important was violently pushed aside, as three billion years of memories flashed out of her subconscious, with all the power of a solar flare.

There was nothing in the world now but the two of them. Sebastian and Mara's minds were so intimately linked, nothing could have separated them. The only thing left was the aching need that had first gripped them, the need to join physically as well as mentally. Their kiss expressed it all; it was the only way left open to them. They didn't have time for anything else.

Gradually, tortuously, they found the strength to let reason return.

They had an unpleasant job to do, one that couldn't wait, and they needed to get on with it.

Breaking apart, their eyes shimmered with increased energy, their skin trembling under its coating of electric charge. Sebastian was the first to speak, his voice rough and self-mocking. "I guess this means we should hold on to our seats. With this much excess energy, we'll be breaking the land speed record!"

Mara giggled. She caught sight of herself in the passenger side mirror. Her eyes swirled with molten gold, desire turning them brighter than ever. Her skin was flushed and her lips swollen. Smiling at her reflection, mischief broke through the sexual haze.

She tightened her seat belt.

"Bring it on, Sebastian, the sooner we do this, the sooner we get this meeting over with."

She paused, before adding huskily, "And the sooner we can be alone."

He gave her a quelling look, his arousal prominent as he eased himself fully back into his seat. He grimaced, with obvious discomfort, before starting the engine and moving out onto the road.

Mara smiled. If she had to feel frustrated, it was only fair that he should as well.

He was right too, the car responded to the additional electricity they'd created. It ran faster and smoother than ever.

They didn't quite break the land speed record, but they did pull up outside 'The Tea Cosy' in record time.

Mara glanced at the door of the café with more than a little apprehension, "So this is it. At least we'll be able to let Alexa go back home now. If Ross is anything like you, he must be going berserk, knowing she's here alone."

Sebastian swung towards her, his expression wary and a little shocked. "What did you just say?"

Puzzled, she repeated herself, "I said that we'll be able to let Alexa go back home now…"

He shook his head, "No, what did you say *after* that?"

"Well, um, I said that I thought Ross might be going berserk…" Her voice trailed off as she watched the shock on Sebastian's face change into something that resembled suspicion. She couldn't be sure though. He was being very careful, keeping his mind blank, and effectively shutting her out. "What's wrong?" She whispered.

He went rigid at her question, his face and mind unreadable. Except… she got a flash of something, swiftly pushed clear of her. Anguish? Guilt?

She watched him, every bit as careful as he was. She hoped she was being successful at keeping her thoughts hidden, because something had alarm bells screaming through her mind.

Then Sebastian did something that Mara knew was a struggle for him. She found that she was reading him much better. The smile that he plastered across his face jarred on her as she waited for the inevitable.

He was going to lie to her.

"Nothing is wrong, my love. Don't look so worried. We really should be getting inside though. I'm sure Jennie will feel calmer once she sees that you're here, and I need to talk to Alexa privately. I'm hoping she's managed to find out some information on the electricity company."

Mara wasn't sure how to handle such a blatant lie. It was obvious that Sebastian believed her to be unaware of what he was doing and, although hurt; her gut reaction was to keep her mouth shut and her eyes open.

Something was definitely wrong. Something he wasn't prepared to tell her.

There was no way she'd let him get away with *that* though. Whether he liked it or not, she needed complete honesty from him. She decided to bide her time.

Smiling at him, she swung her legs out of the car, having barely waited for him to come and hold her door open, before walking over to the café door and stepping through it. Determination swelled inside her.

Whatever was waiting for her, she'd meet it head on. She'd spent too many years in the dark, not knowing about her family or her heritage. There was no way she was going to let Sebastian return her to the oblivion of not knowing. However well intentioned.

CHAPTER 14

Jennie was in front of her as soon as she stepped through the café door, “Oh, Mara! I’m so glad you’re here.”

Shocked, she automatically returned her friend’s hug, wrapping her arms around Jennie. She could hardly believe how much had changed, for both of them, in the last few days.

It was several minutes before Jennie calmed down. Mara guided her over to one of the tables, and then pushed her down into the chair that Sebastian held out for her. She took the one directly opposite, all too aware of the man who hovered between them, watchful, protective.

It meant a lot to her, that he wanted to protect Jennie too.

“Of course I’ll protect her. She’s your friend. A closer friend than I think you realised. I owe her. She cared for you, in her own way, when I could not.”

His words, softly spoken in her mind, caused a shiver of awareness along her spine. *How am I supposed to stay focused, when he’s whispering things like that?* It took determination to turn her attention back to Jennie.

She looked dreadful; her normally smiling face was make-up free and blotchy, from what must have been hours of crying. Her hair, out of its usual ponytail, was nothing short of wild. It looked like she’d continuously run her fingers through it, tugging it in all directions.

Mara leaned forward and rested her hand on Jennie's arm. "Tell us everything that's happened so far. You look scared, Jennie. Surely the electricity company hasn't really threatened you?"

Her friend sniffed, before taking the handkerchief Sebastian held out to her.

Mara eyed the square of cotton. *Where did he get that from?*

"It's a talent of ours. You'll have the knowledge yourself somewhere, but I'll show you how it works. The handkerchief is cotton, which was once living matter, using solar power for photosynthesis, which means..."

"Stop!" There was no way she could take this in right now.

She heard him chuckle in her head, and turned her full attention back to Jennie.

She was dabbing at her eyes, and then blew her nose loudly. "Threatening me is exactly what they're doing. Alexa's been great, don't get me wrong, I'd have fallen to pieces by now if it wasn't for her, but it's still been horrible. They've accused me of all sorts of things.

"They added up the energy consumption of all my kitchen equipment, you know. Apparently, that little exercise was to show me how much electricity I *should* have been using, as opposed to how much I *have* been using. The difference was staggering, Mara. They're convinced that you, I or both of us have been rigging the electric meter. They're so sure; they even went to my home, to check everything was as it should be there."

"And was it?" Mara knew what the answer was, but felt she should ask. It would seem strange if she didn't.

Jennie sniffed again, rubbing the end of her nose with Sebastian's handkerchief. "Yes it was. That's when they looked into *your* energy consumption. They told me they'd found some irregularities, and had a number of questions regarding recent readings from the cottage. They said something about there being 'a marked decrease'. But then, they also mentioned a power spike. It sounded as if they thought you were responsible, as it came from your address. Apparently, it was big enough to take out several thousand pounds worth of cabling and equipment further along the network." She drew in a ragged breath, raking her hand through her hair at the same time, demonstrating how it had got into such a mess. "This is a nightmare."

Mara was at a loss. What could she say? Instinct made her turn her head; to look at the one person she trusted to help.

Sebastian stared back at her. He was still shielding his thoughts. For one agonising moment, his expression was solemn, and she began to fear the worst.

Then he winked.

Relief flooded through her. *"What do I say, Sebastian? I've never seen Jennie like this in all the years I've known her. It breaks my heart to think I'm responsible. She has such a big heart; no one like her should ever have to go through something like this!"*

Tears threatened. Even in her mind, Mara could hear the fear in her words.

Sebastian moved closer. He bent towards them, laid a hand on their shoulders. His hands gave off a subtle flow of heat. It instantly seeped into tense muscles, giving them no choice but to relax. His voice, when it came, was almost hypnotic.

"Listen to me, both of you. There is absolutely nothing for you to worry about. I want you to make yourselves a hot drink and wait for me here. I need to confirm one or two things with Alexa and then make some phone calls, but I'll be back soon. Then I'll tell you exactly how we're going to tackle this. Okay?"

Jennie nodded, but Mara stared at Sebastian hard. He was still lying, but there was something else too. His attitude was different. He looked supremely confident, but she couldn't think what had happened to cause the change.

"Sebastian?" She still felt uncertain and a little frightened. The situation they were in could easily slide into disaster.

A smile flitted across his face, his eyes sparking for a moment as he reached out a hand to cup Mara's face in his palm. *"Trust me Mara. You helped me figure this out, my clever girl. Now you have to have faith in me, faith that I'm right and that I can sort this."*

She shivered slightly, as Sebastian dropped his hand and turned to walk over to where Alexa stood, in the corner of the café, waiting for them to finish talking to Jennie. The place where his hand had rested tingled with warmth and a small pulse of electricity.

Feeling dazed, Mara became aware that Jennie was no longer at the table. Looking around for her, she spotted her in the kitchen. She was keeping herself busy, making a pot of tea.

Alexa and Sebastian were having what looked like a heated conversation; their voices were too low for her to hear. Her link with Sebastian was next to useless at the moment.

Alexa was facing her. Mara's insides knotted as she watched her beautiful face contort, moving from outraged anger and denial, into panic, and then fear. The last emotion she witnessed was the hardest to take. Something akin to remorseful grief filled the other woman's eyes. Tears flowed, as her entire body sagged against the café wall.

If ever there was a picture of despair, Alexa Munroe was it.

Mara's heart immediately went out to her. From the set of his shoulders, she knew that Sebastian was furious about something. Tired of being shut out, Mara pushed her new talents to the max. Maybc she couldn't hear what they were saying, but she should be able to hear the echo of the conversation in his mind, as it was being spoken and heard.

She just had to be ruthless and push her way past the mental block he'd erected.

"You should have trusted me Alexa, you should have told me!" Every syllable was enunciated in a short, clipped voice that barely concealed Sebastian's anger. They were the only words she caught; before he swung round, his eyes widening as he stared her.

Oops. Looked like he knew what she was up to. She decided to go on the defensive, *"Well, what did you expect? You told me we're partners. That means we share everything, not just the good times. Don't keep me out of this, Sebastian. I've lived with secrets for too many years."*

His eyebrows rose at her tart reprimand. Then he gave her one of his 'barely there' smiles, the ones he used to try and charm his way out of bother. Boy, did she remember *those.* Her new memories were peppered with them. He had a cheek, trying to wrangle his way out of this one.

His smile broadened, *"I'm not trying to wrangle my way out of anything, my Mara. Please, have patience. Let me take care of this. It's the only way I can take care of you, as I promised your Father I would."*

"But I need to know what's going on, Sebastian!" Mara was beginning to feel angry as well as frustrated.

"I asked you to trust me. Is that really so difficult?" He sounded impossibly calm.

Mara felt like she was going to explode, hating the fact that he wouldn't connect with her, wouldn't share his emotions or his plans. *"Yes, I mean no… oh hell, I don't know. Please, just talk to me will you? I can't take not knowing."*

She didn't expect him to back down. He was in full *He-man* mode. She didn't know how to reach him, to make him understand.

From across the room she saw his shoulders rise and fall, on a sigh. Then he did something unexpected. He walked towards her, leaving Alexa in the corner. The woman looked as if she was on the point of falling down; her body was shaking so badly.

Coming to stand in front of her, Sebastian hauled her to her feet. For a moment he stared at her, his expression suggesting some sort of internal struggle. Then he kissed her.

In a heartbeat, she felt her mind whirl. He had one hand anchored against the back of her head, giving her no way of escape, whilst his other hand pressed against her lower back, moulding her to him.

Her response was dramatic.

After what had happened in the car, it was as if her body and mind were hard-wired into his needs and emotions. A single touch and the connection between them roared into life.

Electricity, out of control, poured out of them. It swirled around the café's interior in a glowing mist, brightening every light already on, lighting those that weren't. Every kitchen appliance hummed.

Dazed, Mara could only cling to Sebastian, as he slowly raised his head. His eyes glowed with satisfaction. *"Now that should get their attention, my love. You want to know what's going on? Then I'll explain. But first we need to wait for a phone call. I don't think we'll be waiting long for that interview..."*

As if it had been choreographed, she heard the café phone begin to ring, just as Jennie dropped the teapot she'd been holding. Frowning, and still a little bemused by Sebastian's kiss, Mara turned her head to look at her friend.

Jennie was standing in the kitchen doorway, the remains of the teapot scattered around her feet, her face a picture of disbelief. "My God," she whispered, "It *is* you, *both* of you...."

Mara groaned, burying her face in Sebastian's shoulder, "Yes, I'm afraid it is. I'm sorry Jennie. My only defence is that, at the time, I didn't know what I was doing." Her voice was quiet, barely audible. She was convinced that Jennie would condemn her, condemn both of them, for the chaos she'd inadvertently caused.

It came as a shock when she felt a hand on her shoulder. It wasn't Sebastian's.

The phone was still ringing, insistent, in the background but Mara didn't care. Turning her head, she was stunned to see Jennie *smiling* at her. It was just a tiny curl to the lips, but wonderful to see.

Jennie's voice was steady, without a hint of hysteria. "Oh, I'll forgive you eventually. I won't pretend to understand what this is all about but, for now, I'm going to trust you. You are *so* going to fix this, Mara Austin!"

Jennie's hand gently squeezed Mara's shoulder. Then she turned to pick up the phone, her voice was quiet, but tremor free as she answered it. Her eyes never left them.

"Good evening, The Tea Cosy. How can I help you?"

There was a pause, as Jennie listened to the person on the other end of the line. Mara let her eyes sweep the café, taking in her friend's calm expression, Sebastian's stillness as he continued to hold her close, and Alexa, slumped into a chair in the darkest corner of the café.

"Yes, I understand." Jennie replaced the phone into its cradle.

What she said next hardly surprised them.

"They want to see you, Mara. Tonight. It would appear that the employees of my electricity supplier work later than most…" Jennie allowed herself another small smile, "If I wasn't so terrified; I'm sure I'd be impressed!"

Sebastian chuckled, the sound rumbling through his chest. Mara tore her eyes away from Alexa to stare up at him questioningly. "How on earth can you *laugh* Sebastian, don't you know how serious this is?"

He looked down at her, his expression eager, "Oh, don't get me wrong, I know this is serious; the difference is I don't consider it *dangerous*. Not anymore. You see," he paused, to flick a glance in Alexa's direction, "I now have inside information about this situation and access to all the back-up I need."

Mara frowned. "I don't suppose you're going to explain that remark any time soon?"

"Not a chance. But don't worry; I'm learning. I'm prepared to share what I know with you, I just need to make a couple of phone calls before we set off."

"And what am I supposed to do, whilst you make your phone calls? Twiddle my thumbs?" Mara asked.

Sebastian raised his eyebrows at the sarcasm that laced her words, and then he grinned, not in the least bothered by it, "Perhaps you'd like to help Alexa? We're going to need her with us and I don't want either her behaviour or her running make-up to cause us a problem." His expression grew hard as he fished out the mobile phone from his pocket and began to tap in a phone number.

As the call connected, he dropped an absent-minded kiss on the top of Mara's head, his attention obviously elsewhere, and let her go, heading towards the café door.

"If you leave me with Alexa, I'm going to ask her about all this. You know that, right?" Mara asked, staring after him.

He halted for a moment and turned to look back at her. *"I wouldn't expect anything else. You've made your point, Mara. You need to be part of this. Now, stop interrupting me. I have work to do."*

"Yes, Sir." She replied, laughing gently as he grimaced at her, before spinning on his heel and disappearing through the door. She heard him on the phone, as it swung shut behind him.

"Nathan? Right, listen carefully; I need you to get hold of Liam and Joseph. The three of you are taking a trip to Houston, and it's not a visit to our offices…"

Left behind, the three women stared at each other in awkward silence.

Alexa, still cowering in the corner, turned away first. Her eyes were wide and tear filled.

Mara crossed the distance between them. She took a chair close to the distraught woman. "What's wrong, Alexa?" She asked gently.

Jennie followed her lead, pulling up another chair, her hand automatically reaching out to take Alexa's. The other woman immediately tried to tug it away, but Jennie was having none of it.

"Whatever it is, it's not worth getting this upset over. Why don't you tell us about it? We're good listeners, you know." Jennie's voice was low and coaxing and Mara couldn't help the smile that welled up inside her. How many times had Jennie managed to wheedle secrets from her, with that exact same tone of voice? Never mind a good listener, Jennie would make a good psychiatrist.

At first, Alexa wouldn't look at them, but Jennie was determined. After sitting in silence for a few minutes, with Jennie refusing to give up her hold on Alexa's hand, they at last got what they wanted.

She didn't lift her head, but she did begin to talk.

Her voice wavered, as if on the point of breaking. "Oh, it's definitely worth getting this upset over. I've failed my family and I've done something unforgivable, in the eyes of all Lifelights.

"I've sided with the enemy and conspired to hand over one of our own."

CHAPTER 15

It was pretty obvious which Lifelight Alexa was referring to. Mara couldn't help the shiver that ran along her spine; so much for being part of a global, long-lost family. It seemed that some of them were less than enthused to have her back.

More than that though, Alexa was making Jennie aware that there were more Lifelights out there. After everything Sebastian had told her, about secrecy being of paramount importance, Mara wondered how her new family would react to this latest turn of events.

What would they do when they realised that Jennie knew about them?

Looking across at her friend, she was impressed with how she seemed to be taking everything in her stride. Jennie didn't look in the least bit shocked; instead, her face was filled with sympathy as she continued to stare at Alexa, her thumb rubbing across the back of the woman's hand.

Jennie's next words confirmed this, "You don't strike me as the sort of person to betray your own people, Alexa. What could have convinced you to do such a thing, I wonder?" Her voice was thoughtful and with a jolt, Mara realised that she was right.

"They…" Alexa's voice faltered and she took a calming breath before continuing, "They took Ross, my husband; Rosalyn, my daughter, too. They said that they'd force him to kill her, if I didn't help them…" A fresh wave of tears threatened to overwhelm her and Jennie shot Mara a pointed look.

Jumping up, Mara grabbed the box of tissues that was sitting on the café's dresser and thrust them at Alexa. Seating herself again, she watched impatiently as Alexa helped herself to some of the box's contents. She wadded the tissues in her free hand as she tried to stem the flow tears; without much success.

Jennie's voice was gentle as she voiced the exact question that had been battering itself against the inside of Mara's skull.

"But, surely, nothing could ever make a father kill his own child?"

"M… maybe not intentionally, but Ross and I have certain talents, which can be dangerous…." Alexa had finally managed to tug her hand out of Jennie's and was now twisting the tissues round her fingers, "She… she doesn't know about us, you see. She's still too young and she won't understand why her Daddy can't be near her. She'll be so frightened and I can't be there for her, I can't hold her… Please, I would never have said I'd help them, but don't you see? I can't bear for Rosalyn to be frightened and I can't let Ross down. He'd want me to save our daughter - I *have* to save them, both of them!" The last few words seemed to be ripped from Alexa's heart. She stared down at her lap, "I'm so sorry Mara – I had no choice…"

"Oh, you had a choice. You could have trusted in your family, Alexa. You could have come to us for help."

All three women froze at the low, aggressive voice that came from behind them. Mara spun round in her chair to look at Sebastian, who had come back inside the café, his hand raised, fingers still gripping his phone. He'd finished his calls then.

"Sebastian..." Mara's voice was gentle. She rose from her seat and closed the gap between them.

Wrapping her arms around his waist, she leant into him, her head resting on his shoulder. *"Yes, Alexa should have gone to her family for help. But look at her. Do you really believe she's thinking logically?*

"I don't pretend to know who 'they' are, but it doesn't matter. They have her husband and her child, Sebastian. How would you react if someone were to do that to you? How would you feel if someone took me from you – your child from you?"

He stilled against her, in both body and mind. A second later, she felt her chin being pushed upwards, his fingers tipping back her head. She had no option but to look into his eyes. *"I would move heaven and earth to retrieve you, my Mara. Perhaps you're right. Alexa did what she thought was best, in a moment of terror. I still, however, find it hard to forgive her. She wanted to sacrifice you, in return for them. It was the wrong decision."*

"At least tell her you understand that. She's terrified for her family, Sebastian, desperate at the thought of what she's done."

She wound her arms around his neck, pulling him towards her. It was the first time in her life that she'd initiated a kiss. Feeling unsettled and upset, all she could think of was getting as close to him as possible.

It wasn't a passionate kiss. Her body instinctively craved the comfort of his. Her skin tingled as every nerve ending produced a flash of electric charge. Their connection was getting stronger.

The lights around the café flickered, before steadily brightening. She was so used to the subtle flow of electricity, which was always present when they were together, she hardly registered it. Besides, she was far too busy, taking pleasure in this slow, oh so different kiss.

"Hey! You two, cut it out! We have a family to rescue here!" Jennie's voice was sharp and Mara jumped, and then attempted to pull away from Sebastian.

He merely tightened his hold on her and finished their kiss leisurely, as if they had all the time in the world. Lifting his head slowly, he smiled down at her, his eyes full of promise, *"You are so beautiful, my Mara, and you never fail to surprise me. I love that you need me. In fact, I intend to show you exactly how much I love it, as soon as an opportunity presents itself... so far, we've fused only once in this cycle. That's a pitiful track record, by any standard; one that needs rectifying."*

Her breath sped up, as she relived their time at Lochan Fada. For a brief moment, there was only the two of them. But all too soon, reality intruded. She allowed him to move away from her.

Patience was a virtue, or so people said.

He walked over to the two women still sitting in the corner of the café, retaining possession of her hand and pulling her along with him. He wrapped an arm around her as soon as they reached their destination, tucking her against his side before speaking.

"You're right, Jennie; there is much that needs to be done. What can I say? Mara is addictive."

Jennie gave a short laugh, "Funny, to look at her, I'd have sworn that it's *you* that's addictive, Sebastian." She raised her eyebrows at Mara, obviously amused, before swiftly returning to the deadly serious question of Alexa's family. "Now, focus, what are we going to do about Ross and Rosalyn?"

Alexa became still at Jennie's words. Her eyes held a tiny glimmer of hope, as she turned to face Sebastian.

His face stern, eyes empty of emotion, Mara herself would've been scared of him, if she didn't know him better. She gave him a prod in his ribs and frowned at him, tilting her head towards Alexa.

"She made a mistake, Sebastian. One motivated by fear for her family's safety. Don't lose sight of that. You don't have to agree with her decision, but neither should you condemn her."

"I know..." He paused, before speaking out loud, "Alexa, I'll do everything in my power to save your family. That goes without saying. You're a part of my extended family and fall under the protection of all Lifelights." He raised his hand, when she tried to speak, "However, if you *ever* betray us again, put those I love, those Mara loves, in danger… You will be ostracised, banished from the ancient sites until the end of your current human cycle. We have enough dissension to deal with, the Chem…" He glanced at Mara and hesitated, "Let's just say that we have enough trouble to deal with, without worrying that our enemies now have the power to turn us against each other. Do I make myself clear?"

Mara shot him a look. *"Oh, don't for one minute think you got away with that slip-up. You lied to me, Sebastian. You knew that Alexa was hiding something but you still told me there was nothing to worry about. Now you're hiding something else. Not that I'm worried. I have my memories back; it's just a case of sifting through them. But just remember, we're partners. As I've said before, I don't like it when you won't share."*

Sebastian looked back at her calmly, the only sign that he'd heard her being the sudden tightening of his shoulders and jaw. He inclined his head, *"Noted."*

Then he spoke, his voice deliberately calming, "Right, time to talk tactics. This problem requires a two pronged attack," he explained, "We'll meet with the electricity company here in England and remove the threat to Alexa's family in America. After seeking further information, it's as I feared, this isn't a localised threat. However, I have measures in place, ready and waiting for us to make a move; we're free to begin at any time."

"So, we're *all* going to this meeting?" For the first time, Jennie sounded less than confident. The visits she'd received already had obviously frightened her, more than she'd let on.

Sebastian shook his head. His eyes warmed as they rested on Jennie. Mara could feel his growing affection for her. He viewed her as family, just as she did.

"No, *you're* going to stay here, where a friend of mine can keep an eye on you. There's something I want you to consider and discuss with him."

Jennie looked puzzled, as Sebastian raised his phone once more and spoke into it quickly. "We're about to leave, would you join us, Paul?"

The door of the café opened almost immediately and a tall, smartly dressed man, complete with briefcase, stepped through it. Apart from his height, he was the exact opposite to Sebastian in looks. His hair was a deep corn gold, shot through with pale, sun-bleached highlights; his eyes were a dark nut brown. He was also noticeably tanned. It gave the impression of someone who spent a great deal of time outside, at odds with his smart office attire. His business-like suit, crisp shirt and tie, and shiny black shoes screamed 'desk-bound professional'.

Mara, surprised to see someone so obviously human, found herself turning to Jennie, to see what she made of him.

One look at her friend's face, and she had to bite her bottom lip to stop herself smiling. Jennie's eyes were glued to the man as he came further into the café, her expression stunned. Mara heard her draw in a quick breath, before whispering a reverent "Oh boy".

That did it. Mara chuckled softly. Jennie, once again, was smitten.

Seemingly unaware of the stir that Paul was causing, Sebastian stepped forward to shake his hand, before turning to introduce him to them. "This is Paul Weston, my Solicitor here in England. Paul, this is Jennie, the friend I told you about." Sebastian turned to Jennie. "I want you to stay here with Paul, whilst the rest of us go to the meeting. He has some proposals that I'd like you to give careful consideration to. They regard your current business location. I'm sorry to say this, but you may need to think about moving The Tea Cosy. The people making life difficult for Mara and I, could easily extend their harassment to you.

"It's my intention to take Mara back to America with me, and I want to know that you're safe. You *will* listen to Paul, won't you, Jennie?"

Jennie nodded, but Mara seriously doubted that she was actually listening to Sebastian. She also doubted whether Jennie was capable of concentrating on anything Paul had to say. Then again… she glanced at Paul and smirked. The expression on his face, as he came forward to shake Jennie's hand, suggested that he wouldn't fare much better. 'Pole-axed' wasn't a bad description for how he looked, as he forgot to release Jennie's hand and they just stood there, staring at each other.

Looking at Sebastian, she caught a sense of 'something', together with a look of deep satisfaction in his eyes. She stared at him with startled suspicion, *"You wouldn't be playing matchmaker would you, Sebastian?"*

His face was the picture of innocence as he looked down at her. *"Me? Don't be ridiculous; I have enough trouble getting my own woman to come to me, without worrying about pairing anyone else up."*

She remained unconvinced, *"Uh, huh, so why the smug look?"*

He shrugged, *"I'm just pleased that Paul was free this evening, to discuss things with Jennie. He's a very successful and busy man, you know."*

"Of course you are, and of course he is," Mara thought, rolling her eyes at him. Then she deliberately spoke out loud, having noticed that Alexa had used the time taken on introductions to repair her make-up and fix her hair. "So, are we ready to leave? You do know where this meeting is taking place, don't you?"

Both Sebastian and Alexa nodded in reply. "Okay, I suppose we'd better get going then." Mara turned briefly to wink at Jennie, who blushed prettily. She'd taken a seat at one of the tables, Paul sitting next to her. "Guess we'll see you two later. Don't do anything I wouldn't..." She directed this final comment at Jennie, in an overly dramatic whisper.

If possible, her friend's face turned even redder. She glared at Mara, as Sebastian tugged her out of the café. Alexa followed close behind.

CHAPTER 16

The offices of Synergy Electricity Ltd looked just the same as every other office block; Benign.

As Sebastian pulled up in front of reception Mara could see that, apart from the reception area itself, the only room fully lit was on the top floor of the building.

After helping her out of her seat, Sebastian did the same for Alexa. Then he offered Mara his arm. They entered the building smiling. It was a show of solidarity, despite the underlying nerves.

Well, nerves on Mara and Alexa's part. Sebastian appeared as confident as ever.

The security guard at the reception desk showed no surprise at their late visit. He passed over the Visitors book, waited for them to sign it, and directed them to the lifts. He then told them that Mr. Simmons and Mr. Jameson were waiting for them on Floor 10, the last office on the right.

On the short journey up to the tenth floor, Sebastian explained his plan. "Right, Alexa, I want you to act exactly as you would have if we weren't aware of your involvement with this company. This is three against two, but as far as these *gentlemen* are concerned, it's three against two in *their* favour." He paused, to glance down at Mara, "I hope your acting skills are up to scratch? I need you to be shocked and hurt when Alexa's duplicity is revealed. I want these men to be completely at ease. They mustn't suspect a thing. Can you do that for me?"

She nodded, glancing at Alexa, whose complexion had grown ashen under her newly applied make-up.

Nerves fluttered in her stomach as she contemplated what they were about to do. It wouldn't take much to give the impression she was scared witless.

The doors of the lift slid open and the three of them stepped out into a dimly lit corridor, bordered by offices. It was easy to see the office they were headed for. It was the only one with its door open and the lights on.

Mara took a deep breath and tightened her hold on Sebastian's arm.

"Courage, my love, we are forewarned and forearmed. In truth, there really isn't anything to worry about. Just answer their questions and leave the rest to me." Sebastian's thoughts were as soft as down, gently easing her anxiety.

She still couldn't relax though. The thought of Alexa's family, especially her daughter, brought tears to Mara's eyes. Probably a good thing; it added to her overall look of panic.

All too soon, they were standing in front of the office. Sebastian knocked firmly on the open door, his face taking on a set, arrogant expression as he escorted Mara inside. Alexa followed them, the picture of easy elegance.

The office was typical of all the other offices that Mara had ever been in. The floor was covered in tightly woven, dark grey carpet tiles and the space filled with nondescript, hard-wearing furniture. It was the sort of furniture that appealed to company decorators the world over, offering bland versatility for little cost.

The walls of the office were covered with various framed photographs and certificates, set against magnolia walls. The obligatory strip lighting flickered above them.

The two men waiting for them looked far removed from the evil masterminds that Mara had envisioned. One man leant against a filing cabinet in the corner of the room, whilst the other was seated behind the desk. They were almost as nondescript in appearance as the office furniture. Both were in their late forties, perhaps early fifties and average in every respect; medium height, short mousy brown hair, dark pinstriped suits, white shirts and inoffensive ties.

Company men through and through; loyal to the firm if the pay was right, a car and health package forthcoming and the pension benefits reasonable.

Mara detested them on sight.

There was only one chair in front of the over-large desk and the desk lamp was angled slightly towards this. Mara shivered, it wouldn't take much to turn the harmless office into an interrogation room.

She took the seat, grateful that Sebastian was with her. He stood behind her, his hand resting on her shoulder.

The man behind the desk looked mildly surprised; as he watched the three of them enter. He stood-up as they settled themselves, reaching across the desk, in an attempt to shake Mara's hand.

She ignored the gesture. There was no way she'd willingly let either of these men touch her.

The other man remained leaning against the filing cabinet, arms crossed in front of him and a surly expression on his face. *So, that's how it is. We're going to play 'Good Cop, Bad Cop'.*

The first man withdrew his hand and seated himself once more. His eyes narrowed as he regarded the three of them.

Silence stretched out over several moments, until he finally cleared his throat and began to speak.

"Thank you for coming to see us, Miss Austin. I'm Ian Jameson and this is my colleague Patrick Simmons." He paused, nodding to the other man, "Firstly, I'd like to apologise for the lateness of this meeting, but we thought it best to get this over with, especially as you've travelled such a long way to be here.

"I understand that you've been to Scotland? May I ask; was your visit for business or pleasure?"

Mara raised her eyebrows, slightly taken aback by the 'chit chat'. Was this meant to put her at ease? If it was, it wasn't working. "A bit of both, Mr. Jameson, although I'm not sure what that has to do with this interview? I understood that you wanted to see me about my domestic electricity consumption?"

Ian Jameson leant forward, propping his elbows on the desk in front of him and lacing his fingers. He stared thoughtfully at Mara over the top of them. "Ah yes, your energy consumption, that is indeed why we've called this meeting, Miss Austin. However, before we get on to that, perhaps you'd be good enough to introduce your companions?"

Mara's smile was polite, "Yes, of course, I didn't mean to be rude. This is Mr. Sebastian Oran, who accompanied me to Scotland and his Personal Assistant, Ms. Munroe."

It was Patrick Simmons who spoke next, "Sebastian Oran… Is that the same Sebastian Oran who owns Oran Industries in the U.S.?"

Sebastian moved slightly, placing a hand on each of Mara's shoulders. His reply was relaxed and steady. "The very same, Mr. Simmons, and I think I should tell you now; Miss Austin and I have recently become engaged. So, I'd be grateful if you'd come straight to the point. What, exactly, is Synergy Electricity accusing my fiancé of?"

The two men looked at each other for the first time. Their expressions sent a shiver along Mara's spine. She felt Sebastian squeeze her shoulders. *"Courage, my love, trust me."*

"I do trust you, Sebastian; it's these jokers I'd happily feed through the shredding machine."

The chuckle that flitted through her mind relaxed her. She really shouldn't be so nervous; she just wanted this meeting to be over.

Turning back to them, Ian Jameson attempted a smile.

"The allegation is fraud, Mr. Oran. We've reason to believe that your fiancé has been tampering with the electric meters at both her home and work addresses. Significant discrepancies have come to light, that require further investigation."

"Really?" Sebastian managed to sound astonished, "And you have evidence of this?"

Patrick Simmons's smile was a carbon copy of his colleague's. "Oh yes, Mr. Oran, we have proof. We certainly wouldn't waste your time or ours if we didn't. I think you'll find that the figures we've gathered speak for themselves.

"I understand your concerns regarding this, of course. As I recall, you yourself were 'falsely' accused of something similar. However, this time I can assure you, no mistake has been made." He paused to take a breath but before continuing, but Ian Jameson cut in.

"Perhaps you should ask your Personal Assistant to ring your company Solicitors, Mr. Oran. The adverse publicity from cases such as this can be far reaching. I'd hate for Oran Industries to get caught up in any scandal."

Not being able to see Sebastian's expression was driving Mara crazy. *"Steady... this is what we've been waiting for."* His calm, confident voice was exactly what she needed to hear. Steeling herself, she smiled sweetly at the two men.

"You're right, of course. I too would hate for that to happen." She tilted her head back, so that she could look up at Sebastian. "Get Alexa to contact your legal team, darling. There's no need for Oran Industries to get caught up in this, and you know how easily stories like this find their way into the papers."

Sebastian smiled down at her, "Perhaps you're right." He turned to Alexa, "Get onto it would you? The sooner this misunderstanding is sorted out, the better it will be for everyone." His tone was dismissive as he spoke, making it clear that he expected her to follow his instructions immediately.

Alexa made her move. She pulled out her phone and began to enter a number, then appeared to change her mind. Snapping the phone shut, she strolled around the side of the desk and stood next to Patrick Simmons. She stared at him for a moment, and then turned to Sebastian, shaking her head.

"I don't think so, Mr. Oran. You see, this meeting is about far more than your fiancé's electricity bills. They also have some rather interesting information regarding yourself and a number of your employees in the U.S. Synergy U.S.A is the parent company of Synergy Electricity Ltd. They've been gathering evidence against Oran Industries for quite some time." she explained.

Sebastian's facial expression didn't change. There wasn't so much as a flicker, to hint that he knew they were in trouble. He merely leaned his head slightly to one side, his eyes capturing and holding Patrick Simmons' gaze.

"You seem to know my Personal Assistant already Mr. Simmons. Perhaps you and your colleague should dispense with this charade. Are you really interested in Miss Austin, or is it Oran Industries that you've set your sights on?"

It looked as though Patrick Simmons would give anything to break eye contact with Sebastian. Mara saw sweat begin to rise, pinpricks of moisture decorating his brow. She wondered if Sebastian had perfected some way of inhibiting human movement, making it impossible for the man to turn away. It wasn't such a mad idea. Muscles give off electrical impulses, which she supposed could be used by someone like Sebastian, or any Lifelight with a talent for electricity.

She watched as Patrick tried to swallow. The movement of his throat seemed laboured. His answer, when it came, was pushed through lips that wouldn't easily cooperate.

"You can cut the innocent act, Mr. Oran. You may have dodged the bullet once, but your times up. You're a talented man, as are your associates. Synergy U.S.A. is eager to discuss how those talents can best be utilised, including Miss Austin's. I'm sure we can work out a mutually beneficial agreement."

Sebastian smiled. It wasn't nice. His eyes left Patrick to look across at Ian, who hadn't moved a muscle since Alexa had made her move.

"I'd have more faith in the 'mutually beneficial' aspect of that statement, if you *hadn't* involved an innocent girl and her father in our 'discussions'," he commented, ignoring the look of shock that passed between Patrick and Ian, "Yes, I know all about that. However, I'm willing to overlook that, and possibly work with you, if you have the evidence you say you have about.... us."

The two men suddenly seemed to sag, as Sebastian turned his gaze on Alexa. There was a look of relief on their faces as they rolled their shoulders and stared hard at him. *Did he really just paralyse them?* Mara wondered.

"Not totally."

Ian had got some of his courage back. His expression was triumphant as he straightened up in his seat. "Oh, we have evidence. Synergy U.S.A. was handed it on a plate. It would seem that someone doesn't like you, Mr. Oran."

Mara glared at Alexa. "*You're* responsible for this! How could you sell your soul to these people? How could you *do* that to us, Alexa?" She let her acting ability run wild, making sure that disgust, for everything Alexa had done, coated each word.

Alexa's guilt was evident in every line of her body. She stared, white faced, at Mara and Sebastian. Her eyes shone with unshed tears as she whispered her regret. "I'm *so* sorry. But it wasn't me, not at first. They gave me no choice, they…"

Ian gave a delicate cough, his eyes on Alexa. At the same time Patrick's harsh voice filled the office. "That's enough. I'm sure your boss and his fiancé don't need to know the reasons for your betrayal."

Alexa shuddered, "But…"

Patrick's lips curled, his eyes were merciless as he stared at her. "No 'buts' my dear, you did what you did and we are extremely grateful to you. Perhaps you'd like to make that 'phone call we promised you?"

Mara could have cheerfully torn the man limb from limb. Knowing what she did, that these men were involved with the taking and holding of Alexa's family, the hatred she felt towards them became intense. Thoughts of violence threatened to overwhelm her.

"Steady, Mara, our time will come. Just a little longer."

Listening to Sebastian, Mara forced her breathing to slow and her calmer side to re-assert itself. She was under no illusions though; it was a thin veneer of control.

Alexa took the phone that Patrick held out to her. Her hand shook. "Ross?" Her voice trembled with emotion, fingers curling tightly around the phone as she listened to the man speaking to her, "and you're both okay, you *and* Rosalyn?"

The relief that crossed her face was heart-breaking, but as she opened her mouth to say something else the phone was abruptly taken from her. Patrick had snatched it back into his keeping. His voice was clipped as he took over the conversation, "That's enough, thank you, Ross. Now, perhaps you'd be good enough to pass the phone to Julian for me?" There was a brief pause as Ross complied. At the same moment, Patrick sealed his own fate.

He drew a gun from his pocket and pointed it at Alexa.

Ian did the same, his trained on Mara.

Patrick's voice was the only sound in the office, "Julian? Yes, we have them here.

"Lock the cage and meet us at the airport. We're bringing them in. The plane is already waiting; you can tell Mr. Cameron that we'll be with him in a few hours."

He disconnected the phone, his smile smug as he regarded the three of them.

Alexa was the first to speak, "But, you said you'd let them go if I helped you. Please, you can't lock them up again. Ross won't be able to control himself, he'll *kill* Rosalyn!"

The two men laughed.

The horror in Alexa's voice, the sound of Patrick and Ian's laughter, was too much for Mara. Anger exploded out of her in a deadly wave, just as Alexa's own feelings overwhelmed her.

Electricity and microwaves - a fatal combination.

The acrid smell of burning tissue filled the room, as both men dropped their weapons.

They clutched at their heads. Blood vessels burst, as their eyes stretched impossibly wide, rolling back into their skulls. Their mouths became fixed in the grimace of silent screams. Agony contorted their faces as they were seared from the inside out. Internal organs destroyed, blood cooking within veins, fat deposits exploding with heat, rupturing skin, like sausages bursting on the grill. Then finally everything that covered them, skin, hair, clothes, burst into flames.

It took less than a minute for two lives to end, in a blaze of pain and terror.

Mara froze. Her eyes widened with shock. She stared at the figures in front of her. So still. One lay stretched out on the floor, the other across the desk. Her eyes found Alexa.

Horror stared back at her.

What had they done?

Only Sebastian seemed unmoved by what had happened. He came from behind Mara, to survey the bodies. His face was expressionless.

The next moment he had his phone open and was speaking into it quietly. Authority infused his words.

"Nathan, I'm afraid the people at this end pushed the girls too far. Did you manage to trace where the call was routed to?" He paused for a moment, his eyes flicking between Mara and Alexa. "Good. Make sure the others recognise the urgency, but move carefully. This is what we've been training for, Nathan." His eyes sought

Mara's, but she couldn't bring herself to connect with him, "They're in shock. I'm going to get them out of here as quickly as possible. We'll be with you shortly. I just have to take care of the evidence here."

Mara's brain was incapable of holding onto details. Bits and pieces of information floated into her conscious mind, but most slid past her. She knew that Sebastian was there and that both she and Alexa were safe.

She also knew that there was a fire. It started in an open drawer of the filing cabinet and leaped to the blinds at the office windows. The carpet caught next, the blaze spreading quickly.

The five bodies that the fire service would eventually recover were burnt beyond recognition.

Then Sebastian was pushing her down into her seat in the car, his eyes concerned as they swept over her. Turning her head, Mara could see Alexa, propped up on the back seat, her eyes closed. Briefly she wondered if she was dreaming. If the three of them were here, then how come there'd been five people in the burning office?

It was all so confusing.

The last thing that registered, as the car sped along a darkened road, was the sound of sirens filling the air.

"I love you, my Mara."

So tired; she closed her eyes.

CHAPTER 17

Is that Tea?

Mara struggled to open her eyes as she felt the hot, sweet liquid being coaxed down her throat.

Slowly the lead weights that pinned her eyelids closed grew lighter. She opened her eyes, wanting to see the person who stood over her.

It turned out to be more than one.

Disorientated, she closed her eyes again and counted to ten; then risked another peek.

She was back in The Tea Cosy, cradled in Sebastian's arms. Jennie and another man were bent over her solicitously. Jennie held a teacup and saucer in her hands.

Of course she did. Tea or Coffee was Jennie's answer to most things.

Mara frowned as she fought to remember what had happened to her. The man was… Paul. He was here because… Sebastian had decided he was the perfect person to care for Jennie.

Slowly, snippets of information and memories re-surfaced.

There were visions of a burning office, cloaked in thick smoke. Death, the sight and smell of it, dominated her thoughts.

She closed her eyes and groaned.

She'd killed a man; *two* men. She was a monster, a failure as a Lifelight.

On learning what she was, she'd wanted to embrace her heritage. She'd wanted to be everything that the name of her species suggested - A creature of life and light.

Instead, she'd brought death and darkness.

Mara buried her face in Sebastian's chest, as her body began to shake. Grief and shame weighed her down.

A hand, so gentle, rubbed along her arm in a gesture of comfort. Another came up to cup her chin. Its pressure was insistent, pushing upwards, tilting her head back. Mara kept her eyes shut.

She knew it was Sebastian, but she couldn't bring herself to look at him, couldn't bear for him to see her for what she really was. *A killer.*

"Mara," the sound of Sebastian's voice in her mind tested her resolve, *"Please look at me. I need to see your eyes, my darling; I need to know that you still love me, despite everything I've done to you."* The longing in his words broke through, shocking her.

Her eyes flew open, fixing on the silver gaze focused on her alone.

"Of course I still love you, Sebastian. You've done nothing wrong. I was the one who took two innocent lives."

"Innocent? I think not... those men were ruled by their love of power. It ate away at their souls, until they were corrupted and evil. Did you think they looked civilized in their suits? It was nothing more than an illusion. They were prepared to sacrifice the life of a child, Mara, a girl of eleven years, whose only crime was to be born a Lifelight.

"We crossed a line tonight, my Mara.

"War looms on the horizon. A war between us, the energy industry and, it would seem... a third party; as yet unidentified. I would have given anything to avoid

what happened earlier, what you had to go through, what happens next. We have no option though. We must face the threat to our species head-on.

"Patrick Simmons and Ian Jameson were the first casualties, of something beyond our control.

"I fear they won't be the last." Sebastian's voice was soft and deep. Strong.

She clung to it in her mind. The words couldn't take away the horror of what she'd done, but they helped her to see it from a different perspective. But still… "I should never have lost control."

Sebastian looked at her with understanding. His hand stroked along her hair and face. "Perhaps not, but you are new to this phase of your cycle and have a lot to re-learn. Don't forget, it wasn't only you whose power overwhelmed her. Alexa is an experienced Lifelight and she too lost control.

"No one will ever know what hit those men first. At the moment you stopped their hearts, Alexa melted their internal organs. There was no way that either of them could have survived that. With or without you, they would have died."

Mara shivered. The words, spoken out loud, brought her memories of the office sharply into focus. She couldn't stop the tears.

Sebastian held her. He tucked her into his chest and rocked her gently, allowing her to cry out the guilt and fear. When the sobs began to slow, he tilted her face up to his once more. "I need to go, my Mara."

She struggled into a more upright position.

"Go where, Sebastian?"

She rubbed at her eyes, and then looked around the café. *Where's Alexa?*

Jennie and Paul had retreated to the other side of the room, their chairs pushed close together. They stared across the room at her, their faces showing concern. Paul held one of Jennie's hands, cradling it in his lap. Mara noticed how he gently rubbed the back of it, soothing her friend.

She felt an unexpected feeling of tenderness bubble up inside her. Looking at them she began to wonder if Sebastian was right. Was Paul the man for Jennie? Her friend would need someone close, to rely on, if what Sebastian said was true. If a war loomed between the Lifelights and the energy industry or whoever else had betrayed them, Mara would need to know that Jennie was safe.

Someone was definitely missing from the café though. Even though she knew he must have read her thoughts, Mara turned to Sebastian and repeated her question out loud. "Where's Alexa?"

"In Houston; she's helping to coordinate the rescue of her family." His tone was matter of fact, "Nathan, Liam and Joseph, Lifelights you've yet to meet, are already in position. Now that I'm sure you're well, I'll join them. We must get Ross and Rosalyn away from Synergy U.S.A.'s offices as soon as possible." He paused, as if considering his next words, "I want you to stay here with Jennie and Paul. I know that I told you we must keep our existence a secret, but there are exceptions to every rule. These two are the exception to *this* rule. They are aware of what we are and are now part of our extended family. Their protection has become a priority for all Lifelights.

"Because of this, I'm entrusting them with your safety, Mara. I'll come back to you as soon as I can." Shifting, he rose from the chair and turned, obviously intending to settle her back down on its cushioned seat.

She locked her arms tightly around his neck and refused to let go. Her eyes met his.

"Oh, no you don't, Sebastian. If you're going to Houston, then so am I," Her chin was set, body tensed. There was no way she was staying here in the café.

Not when others were risking their lives.

His eyes narrowed as he assessed the strength of her resolve. She could feel his presence in her mind. He was watching her, her reaction. He made no secret of what he was doing, exploring her thoughts rigorously. When she refused to back down, he sighed, "It's too dangerous. Perhaps, if you were more used to your talents…" his voice trailed off.

Mara let her determination crowd in on him… she wouldn't wait at The Tea Cosy. If he didn't take her with him, she'd try to get there by herself, *and who knows where I'll end up, if left to my own devices?*

She felt his resignation before she heard another long suffering sigh. *Oh yeah, girl power.*

He straightened, Mara still held in his arms. Then he walked over to Jennie and Paul. They stood-up as they approached.

"I'm afraid that I failed to factor Mara's stubborn streak in to my plans. She'll be coming with me."

"Is that safe?" Jennie asked, sounding worried. Her hand gripped Paul's.

"Of course it's not safe," Sebastian said.

Despite his simmering disapproval, Mara knew he wouldn't leave her behind now.

Paul looked almost as disapproving as Sebastian did. He glanced at Jennie before speaking, "Can't say I like the revised plan, but you know best, Sebastian. What do you need me…" he paused. Jennie was visibly squeezing his hand; hard, "Sorry. Let me rephrase that. What do you need *us* to do? Is there anything that we can set in motion from this end?"

"I want you to begin the process of moving The Tea Cosy, as a business, to another location. Think big. It may be best to move to a totally different county or even another country; I know Mara would be delighted if the business moved to America… But wherever it goes, it must be Jennie's decision. Go over the logistics of such a move and contact my offices for a list of suitable premises when you've had time to consider all the options."

Jennie spoke up then, "What about tonight? Am I likely to get a visit from Synergy Ltd any time soon, or the police?"

Sebastian shook his head, "No. As far as the authorities are concerned, five people died in that fire; three men and two women." He didn't seem surprised when Jennie opened her mouth to speak, cutting her off before she got the first word out, "Please, don't ask me to explain that. Unfortunately, we're out of time. The only thing that matters is that they won't be calling."

"But surely they'll come to ask me something about Mara? There'll be a record of who visited the offices tonight. It'll lead the authorities straight to her," Jennie said, remaining unconvinced.

Sebastian shook his head again. "There are no records. Unfortunately, for those investigating the fire that is, a power surge knocked out the security cameras just before we entered the building. Also, I'm rather quick on my feet when I want to be… which reminds me, could you dispose of something for me please?" He nodded with his head towards his coat, abandoned on one of the tables. He would have found it difficult to get it himself, as Mara had wrapped herself around him like a Boa constrictor. She didn't trust him not to vanish if she let go.

Paul walked across to the table and reached for the coat. It soon became clear that it wasn't the coat that Sebastian wanted them to dispose of. Underneath it was a large, thin black book – the visitors' book from Synergy Electricity Ltd.

Raising his eyebrows, Paul whistled softly. He turned back to Sebastian and Mara, "You weren't exaggerating about being quick on your feet. How did you manage to swipe this without the guard seeing?"

Sebastian shrugged, "It wasn't that difficult. The security guard was more interested in the fire alarm. I think everything else was just a blur to him."

Paul's eyebrows climbed even higher, a smile of appreciation curving his mouth, "Hmm, after seeing you in action over the years, I can well believe that you and everyone with you was a blur."

Jennie was looking puzzled. Paul smiled at her reassuringly as he walked back across the café; the visitors' book tucked under one arm. He wrapped his free arm around her shoulders.

The blush that stole across Jennie's cheeks spoke volumes about how she felt about him.

Hugging her closer to his side, he looked up at Sebastian and Mara, "Don't worry; we'll make sure that this book disappears." Then he glanced down, a smile once again tugging at his lips as he looked at Jennie, "And I'll make *sure* that this lovely lady disappears too. Somewhere safe. I take it that time is of the essence with regard to that?"

Sebastian nodded, his grip on Mara tightening, "Yes. There's about to be another discrepancy in The Tea Cosy's electricity readings. A power spike, to be precise.

"I don't expect anyone at Synergy Electricity Ltd to notice it tonight, but they will at some point; I'm guessing sooner rather than later. Both of you need to be gone by then.

"You know where to go if you need help."

Paul nodded, "Of course, Oran Industries or one of its subsidiary companies. Look after yourself, Sebastian… and Mara."

It was Sebastian's turn to smile now, "Oh, don't you worry about that. I have no intention of letting anyone touch *my* woman *or* me. Goodbye for now; we'll see you again soon – both of you."

Before she had a chance to realise that the goodbyes had been said, Mara found herself with a picture in her mind.

A darkened doorway, on a city street; she closed her eyes, realising what it meant and needing to take in every detail.

The colour of the building as it reflected the early evening light, the shine of copious amounts of metal and glass. The smells and the noise of Houston all around them…

A warm wind caressed her skin. Then she was being lowered to the ground.

Her feet made contact with the floor, and one thing became clear.

The Tea Cosy's carpeted floor had disappeared.

CHAPTER 18

Sebastian's arm was wrapped around her waist, his eyes serious as he watched her.

The sign in front of them read 'Synergy U.S.A., 20E Greenway Plaza'. Not that they were outside the main office doorway. It looked more like the entrance to an underground car park.

Mara looked up at him questioningly, *"What makes you think that Alexa and the others are in there?"*

"Because this is where I last contacted Nathan and there is no way the equipment needed to restrain Ross Munroe would be housed in an office suite.

"A hidden room, off a dark underground parking lot, is far more likely."

Mara wondered why she'd bothered to ask. *Yeah, that figures. Cue the scary music.*

She nodded all the same, seeing how it made sense.

She pressed herself closer to Sebastian's side. Although she'd never admit it her heart pounded with fear.

These were the people who'd kidnapped Alexa's family. They'd forced her to betray her people and threatened to kill an eleven year old child.

They were definitely not nice people.

Sebastian let go of her waist and took her hand. He pulled her forward, motioning for her to be quiet. Mara looked up and saw a camera on the wall just inside the parking area. It pointed directly at them. She drew in her breath sharply and pointed towards it.

Sebastian's gaze followed the direction of her hand, his smile humourless. *"Don't worry. Synergy U.S.A. has been without its security cameras for most of the day. Nathan saw to that. They're blind; but that will only make them more dangerous.*

"By now, they have to know we're moving in on them. It won't have taken long for news of the fire in England to reach them... they'll know we'll be coming for Ross and Rosalyn.

"Keep your eyes and ears open. If I was them, reinforcements would be on their way."

Another minute or two, and they were well inside the parking lot. Its darkened interior felt threatening and, no matter how lightly she tried to walk, the echo of her footsteps on the concrete floor seemed overly loud.

At first everything appeared as it should be. But a moment later a tall figure detached itself from the shadows. It slid out from beside one of the pillars supporting the parking lot roof, moving with total silence.

Mara froze in an instant. She nearly collapsed with relief when Sebastian held out his arm in greeting, shaking the man's outstretched hand.

Neither of them spoke. Sebastian used their link to introduce the silent Lifelight.

"This is Joseph. He'll take us to where Ross and Rosalyn are being held. The others are waiting for us there."

She looked at the man with interest, no longer surprised by his appearance. He was tall, well over six feet, with a trim but muscled physique. The only feature she'd have any hope of identifying were his eyes. They were dark green, swirled with the same silver light as

Sebastian's. His clothes were unrelenting black, covering him from top to bottom, his skin disguised by equally black camouflage paint.

It explained why they hadn't spotted him at first. Mara looked enviously at his soft soled boots. They made barely a sound on the parking lot floor.

Joseph moved like a ghost in front of them, beckoning for them to follow him.

Once out of the main lot they passed through a heavy side door that led to a flight of steps. *Of course, they couldn't go 'up' could they?* Mara thought, as they were led deeper underground.

At the bottom of the stairs was another door. It led into a huge, dimly lit space. Stepping through the door, she saw what looked like another level of the parking lot. There wasn't a car to be seen. Instead, a metal container, approximately three metres square, occupied the centre space.

Spotlights and cameras were trained on every angle of it.

"I have a bad feeling about this, Sebastian."

He squeezed her hand, but offered no reassurance, *"With good reason, Mara."*

In front of the container were Alexa, who looked ashen, two Lifelight males that she knew she hadn't met before, and two human men. She assumed that the Lifelights were Liam and Nathan, but there was no time for introductions. Both the humans were built like trucks, but despite their formidable muscle power they were now sitting on the floor in front of the container. Tied back to back; they looked surprisingly confident, given their position.

Mara frowned and looked towards Sebastian, "What is this thing?" She whispered. She was uncomfortable using telepathy in front of the two men.

Sebastian had stepped away from her to inspect the container. He walked around it, touched it, and studied the two keypads mounted to the left of the door. He paid particular attention to the door, which was mounted flush with the metal walls, almost invisible. After a few seconds, his eyes widened and he stepped back.

His expression was calm, but Mara knew different. She could have taken her pick of emotions; horror, shock, fascination, grudging admiration.

"Manual keypads, no electricity involved. Oh, that's very, very clever Mr. Cameron." He murmured, half to himself, before turning back to Mara to answer her question. "This is a variation on the Faraday Cage. Essentially, it works the same as a microwave oven. It keeps those on the outside safe, whilst anyone inside… well, I'm sure you can imagine the effect for yourself."

Mara thought about that for a moment and then felt the colour drain from her face as a silent scream of protest rose up inside her, "Do you mean… do you mean that these people have put Ross *and* Rosalyn inside this thing? But Rosalyn is only eleven - she hasn't matured yet. How long can Ross go without discharging his energy? I thought you said we needed to use our talents regularly, to stop us overloading... but if this doesn't allow him to do that safely... if there's nowhere else for the energy to go… Oh my God."

Sebastian glanced at the men tied up on the floor of the room. His face filled with disgust, "Yes. I think you get the full horror of this setup. That's exactly what they've done." He paused, squatting down to the side of the men, so that he could see their faces. His head tilted one way and then the other. He studied them, "And by the look of those keypads, I'm guessing that these gentlemen possess the number sequences we need.

Which means… all we have to do to open it, is persuade one of them to give us the codes."

The men made the mistake of looking too confident.

Sebastian continued to stare at them in silence for several long moments. His eyes narrowed as he watched them. "Ah, so we need both of you to cough up the information do we? A number sequence for each keypad and neither one of you knows both."

The confident looks faltered.

Sebastian gave them both a smile, of sorts, never taking his eyes off them. "What a shame. It doesn't look like either of you is going to enlighten us, does it? Perhaps you need to be persuaded…"

"Sebastian, what are you thinking of?" Horrified as she was with the situation, Mara could still remember the faces of the men back in England, in the moments before they died. She didn't think she could cope with seeing something like that again.

Sebastian stood up and crossed to her side. His hand reached up to caress the side of her face, his expression solemn. *"You know that we have to do something don't you, Mara? We can't allow Ross to kill Rosalyn and we're running out of time."*

She bowed her head, "I know. I just don't see how we're going to do it in time."

"I can think of a way."

The voice that spoke was deep and resonant. It rumbled through the air in much the same way that it had in Slioch's caves.

There was the sound of weapons being raised, but a sharp command from Sebastian cancelled the reflexive action.

Spinning round, Mara gasped, her eyes widening as they came to rest on her father.

"Daddy… how on earth did you get here?" Without realising it, she addressed him in a voice that he hadn't heard since she was three years old. Marcus's eyes glistened as he recognised the note of hope in his daughter's voice, that her father could somehow help her.

"I got here in just under three seconds, Mara, as you said before; visiting America isn't that difficult. Now, what seems to be the problem, baby girl?"

"But how did you know where I was?" She was struggling to comprehend that her father was really here, standing in front of her.

Marcus reached into the pocket of his jacket and pulled out a mobile phone. He grinned sheepishly. "Ok, I confess, I rang The Tea Cosy to see if Jennie knew anything. She was as confused as hell to be hearing from a dead man and worried sick about you, but she and Paul still gave me the info I needed to find you.

"As I said before, your family has a right to protect you, Mara. I have the right to be here," Marcus's eyes drifted over to the two men, "I have the right to protect you from monsters like these." His gaze then settled on Sebastian, "You said you'd call for help."

Mara felt a tremor of unease, only then becoming aware that her father wasn't alone. A group of ten Lifelights stood rigidly behind him. All looked severe, huge, and were dressed in camouflage gear. They were also armed. *Why would Lifelights need to carry guns?*

"To keep the bulk of their powers secret, if possible," Sebastian explained.

He didn't look remotely concerned by Marcus's arrival. He stood firm under the other man's disapproval. "I called my own people. I knew that their training was everything I needed to get us through this and keep everyone, including Mara, safe." There was no apology for his actions.

Marcus regarded him sternly for a moment longer, and then nodded, "I understand; now, about this problem with the codes."

All eyes turned to the Faraday Cage, but it was Alexa's husky voice that answered, "Please, Marcus, my daughter and husband are in there. I… I don't know how long…" her voice faded, her emotions robbing her of speech.

Marcus nodded again, his face blank. Mara wondered if it was the only way he could deal with the sight of Alexa's desperation.

He turned his attention to the men on the floor. They eyed him warily. "I'll need Mara's help, of course, but this can be done Sebastian. You surely haven't forgotten what she is."

Sebastian's eyes rested on Mara, who was thoroughly confused by the whole conversation, "I haven't forgotten. But, do you think her capable of harnessing that particular talent? I know that it's a talent you share, but although her memories are back, her skills have yet to be honed."

Marcus glared at him, "Her human brain is a rarity; to be treasured, Sebastian. Its power lay unrecognised for too many centuries. Don't perpetuate that mistake. She can do this. *We* can do this."

Mara, who'd had enough of being talked over, opened her mouth to demand that they tell her what they were talking about.

Sebastian placed a hand on her arm, his eyes warm as his gaze touched her face. *"Do not be offended, my love. Your father's right; I should appreciate your strength and talent far more. There is no need for explanations; look into your memories, you already know what is required. I believe in you, my clever girl, and I trust in your expertise. Think, Mara, and harness the skills that your human brain gives you. Let the savant in you help us."*

Not for the first time since she'd met him, Mara felt as though she were in a dream. No sooner had his voice faded from her mind, than she felt her father guide her over to one of the men. He encouraged her to kneel down beside him, and then placed one of her hands on each side of his head. Then Marcus left her, going over to the second man, where he mirrored her position. His eyes closed, as his brow furrowed in concentration. Confused, Mara stared at him for a moment, before turning her attention to the man in front of her. She was unsure of what she was meant to do.

"Remember your skills, Mara. Remember your love of numbers. What was it that Jennie called you, Miss Maths Genius?" Sebastian's voice provided the trigger she needed; memories swam through her, showing her a skill that was rare amongst Lifelights, a skill that was only possible through collaboration. Between her human brain, a perfect copy of a mathematical savant's, and her talent for manipulating and reading electrical impulses.

It was as if an inner voice guided her. Mara allowed her eyelids to become heavy and close. Then her mind went blank, her focus on the man in front of her. She could feel his skin and hair beneath her palms, the warmth that radiated from him. She could hear the rapid beating of his heart, the sound of his breath and the hum of his blood as it flowed through his veins. Then something else began to make its presence felt.

There was a subtle flow of electricity passing through every cell of the man's body. Although it was a product of chemical reaction, it was electricity nonetheless. It was something she understood.

Her breathing deepened, as she followed the path of the electricity, finding the places where it pooled and strengthened. Finally, it led her to the man's brain.

Deep within the Cerebrum, electricity became a glorious, pyrotechnic display. The Nuclei and Dendrites pulsed and glowed with iridescent colour, the flash of the synaptic sparks was breath-taking. Something deep inside her thrilled, her attention arrested by the beauty in front of her. But gradually she felt the pull of information, locked deep within the display itself.

She focused her mind again, began to search through the mass of information that bombarded her, aware that the man was trying his best to confuse and delay her progress. He'd started to think of random number patterns, in an attempt to hide the one she needed.

It was a useless ploy. As focused as she'd become, the insignificant numbers that massed around her faded into the background, the string she was after rose closer to the surface of the man's memories, glowing brightly, rising above the surrounding dullness.

She knew, beyond a doubt, that this man had the sequence to the second key pad. But could she be sure that the numbers she'd found were right? What if she'd made a mistake and confused a six with a nine or thought she'd seen a three when it was an eight. What if she'd discovered the numbers in the wrong order? Fear swelled within her and she hesitated for a moment. If this didn't work, two more lives would be lost. Maybe not in the human sense, but… she realised that she had no option.

Mara opened her mouth and found her voice, reciting the numbers as they'd appeared to her, "3, 6, 2, 2, 9, 1."

It was done.

Unsure of her success, she stared at the numbers still highlighted in front of her. When even these began to fade, she felt an urge to follow where they led, to slip deeper into the beauty of the electrical pulses surrounding her. It would be so easy. Perhaps it would even be better… for everyone concerned. She'd made a mess of this cycle. If she slipped away now, maybe she'd do better next time.

Then she heard him, calling her back. Sebastian.

"Where are you? Come back to me, my Mara. Please…" the words were no more than a trickle of sound against the walls of her consciousness, feather soft.

She responded instantly, blanking out everything but the sound of his voice until, finally, she found her way back. She opened her eyes, once more beside the Faraday Cage, with Marcus next to her and Sebastian's arms wrapped around her, as he gently pulled her into a standing position.

Looking up at him, she was shocked by his expression. He looked… relieved?

Then, as if nothing on earth could have stopped him, he crushed her tightly against him, his mouth claiming hers, pulling her further into the here and now. The kiss and the feelings behind it were as elemental as the electricity she'd just witnessed.

"I thought you were going to leave me."

The thought was an anguished whisper, direct into her mind as she felt his arms tighten around her.

Her denial was silenced before it even reached her lips. *Didn't he understand? It wasn't him she was leaving; it was her failure to be what he needed. The partner he deserved.*

The language and emotion that ripped through her mind stunned her into silence. Her legs failed, as she clung to him, the kiss demanding her complete surrender. But he kept her safe. Nothing else mattered in that moment; until a soft clicking sound, as buttons were depressed, registered in their minds.

The numbers were being entered.

Mara stiffened as she turned to look at the Faraday Cage. *Were they right?*

The breaths of all present stopped.

Sebastian refused to let her go; sending wave after wave of reassurance, that hardly touched her. She watched, fascinated, as Joseph turned to the second keypad and began to enter the numbers *she* had retrieved.

His fingers were steady as he punched in the sequence.

There was a moment's pause, and a click.

Then all hell broke loose.

The door of the Faraday Cage swung open and Liam and Nathan ran inside, just as shouts echoed from the parking lot above.

Joseph spun round and grabbed at Alexa, as she attempted to follow Liam and Nathan into the cage. She kicked and screamed; desperation for her family etched deeply into her tear stained face.

The sound of feet, thundering down the steps from the parking lot above, struck terror into Mara's heart. She watched, wide eyed, as the armed Lifelights met the influx of men that appeared at the doorway.

There was the sound of gunfire.

Light flashed as weapons discharged, first in the stairwell, then nearer, as more soldiers moved in.

Bullets flew everywhere, hitting the concrete pillars, walls and floor. Puffs of dust rose into the air as they became embedded, or glanced off a smooth surface. A shower of high speed metal ricocheted around them.

The noise was deafening.

The Faraday Cage should have been heavily hit, but as Mara watched, she saw something amazing. Its smooth lined walls deflected the speeding missiles with ease.

She gasped, fascinated by the velocity driven ballet of metal, fire and sound.

Her first instinct had been to duck, to curl her body into as small a target as possible, preferably on the floor. But she'd been held in place by Sebastian and Marcus.

"No need to hide," was the only explanation given.

As the battle moved further into the room, it raged around the Faraday Cage with little regard for anyone who stood in its way. Loss of life seemed inevitable.

Only it wasn't.

The Soldiers streaming in to the lower level were intent on causing as much physical damage as possible, whereas the Lifelights fought with greater precision. Their shots were just as prolific, but the placing of them was designed to disable rather than kill.

If Mara hadn't seen it with her own eyes, she wouldn't have believed it.

"Not a single bullet has hit a Lifelight. None have come anywhere near us. How…?"

"Electromagnetic energy. Luckily for us, Mr. Cameron's hired army is using amour piercing steel as their ammunition of choice. Your father came well prepared for this eventuality. Look beside the entrance. What do you see?"

Mara glanced in the direction he indicated… and her eyes widened. Two Lifelights were standing beside the door, one on either side of it. They seemed to be… *conducting?*

It took only a moment for her to realise what they were doing. Electromagnetic displacement; they deflected the steel cased bullets with the flick of a wrist, sending streams of invisible power to every corner of the room.

Mara didn't know where to look or what to do. Her concern for Alexa was rising, but Sebastian and Marcus continued to hold her firm.

One of the Lifelights, she wasn't sure who was who, came running out of the cage, clutching a young girl in his arms. She appeared unconscious.

The bullets twisted around them, like shining confetti as his roar of anger joined the symphony of gunfire. He began to run, full-force, through Lifelights and soldiers alike. A golden glow surrounded both him and the girl. Anyone who came close was pushed violently from their path by an impenetrable barrier. In seconds he'd raced up the stairs and disappeared from sight.

The second Lifelight helped a frail looking man into the outer room. Ross Munroe leaned heavily on his rescuer. He sweated profusely, his skin pallid, even as his eyes swirled with a mixture of silver and blood red light.

As Mara watched, open mouthed, the phrase 'Dead Man Walking' flew into her mind.

So this is Ross... even as she thought it, he swung his head towards them. His eyes settled on Sebastian.

Then his voice, cracked with strain, whispered out. It fell in to a moment of unexpected, unnatural silence.

"Sebastian... please. Get. Everyone. Out."

In the next instant, Mara heard someone screaming… Alexa.

She saw the man's eyes turn to seek out his wife, and the look of exhausted defeat, as his face and body exploded outwards in a flash of bright, white light.

Seconds later, she was back in the caves of Slioch. She had no idea how she'd got there.

CHAPTER 19

Is everyone safe?

Mara made a mental roll-call. Tension held her body immobile as her eyes searched the faces of those closest to her.

It was a relief to realise that she was held against Sebastian. His body formed a solid, protective wall at her back. His arms were wrapped around her waist, filling her with heated reassurance.

She loved to be held like this, the way that they fit together.

A short distance away, she saw her father embrace her mother. They were totally focused on each other. It was a humbling sight.

The others she recognised were Joseph, who looked almost shell-shocked and one of the other Lifelight males, the one who'd helped Ross. She'd have to find out his name. Was he Liam or Nathan? He stood awkwardly to one side, his hand rubbing the back of his neck, his dazed eyes skimming the other Lifelights that had accompanied Marcus. All of them shared the same expression. Deep shock.

There were absences though…

Turning in Sebastian's arms, Mara looked up at him. "Where are the others?" She whispered, "Where are Ross, Alexa and Rosalyn?"

The look in his eyes made her want to retract the question.

His arms tightened around her, pulling her closer, until her face was pressed against his chest, his head resting lightly atop hers. *"There were more casualties, Mara..."*

Denial ripped its way through her, *"NO! Not Rosalyn! Not..."*

Sebastian thrust his response sharply into her mind, *"No, Mara, not Rosalyn and not Nathan. They were well clear before the blast; but Ross, Alexa, Synergy's employees, the hired soldiers.... they were not so lucky.*

"What Ross did was almost miraculous. I find it hard to believe that he held on for so long, to protect Rosalyn. In the end, there was just too much energy, even for him. He couldn't control it. His talent destroyed his human body."

A confusing mix of emotion infused her thoughts. There was relief for Rosalyn, horror for those killed, and a growing need for revenge. In her mind's eye she could still see the effects of her and Alexa's energy discharge, on the bodies of Patrick Simmons and Ian Jameson. She shuddered.

What damage had Ross's death caused? So much energy...

Sebastian gathered her close. Silently they leant each other strength.

It took a moment or two for her to register the phones that had begun ringing in every corner of the cave.

She turned her head, startled, to see what was going on. Lifelights all around her were talking rapidly into their phones. She caught only snippets of the conversations. "Yes, Ross and Alexa…", "Never seen anything like it…", "Must have taken out half of Houston's power grid…", "Have the Italians been informed?" "The Russians are there already?"

Mara understood that what she was hearing was the start of damage limitation, but what was that about *Italians and Russians?*

"Italian and Russian Lifelights," Sebastian whispered, *"And that will be the 'tip of the iceberg' as it were. Lifelights from across the globe have already travelled to Houston. The explosion of energy that Ross's death caused will require an international response if we want any hope of covering it up effectively."*

"But why bother? Synergy U.S.A. will know what caused it," she pointed out.

"Perhaps. I'm starting to wonder though... There's something about this whole set-up that's ringing serious alarm bells."

"No shit, Sherlock."

Her caustic reply produced an answering, welcome, tremor of humour. It slipped silently across her mind, giving her more reassurance than any of the words she'd heard so far.

"What I meant, my love, was that I'm beginning to wonder if Synergy U.S.A. is everything they seem to be. I've yet to meet Mr. Cameron, but so far he's shown a surprisingly high-level of knowledge with regard to our species. Far more than I expected... He knew how to imprison us."

"Well, thank God he didn't know to order in lead bullets." Mara said, shivering. It didn't bear thinking about. How many more Lifelights would have been forced to abandon their human bodies or heal themselves, if the soldiers had used non-magnetic ammunition?

Sensing someone beside them, Mara turned her head to find Joseph standing there. His eyes were huge, shimmering with silver, pain-filled. When he spoke, his voice was raw with emotion, "Sebastian… I tried to keep hold of her… she was determined; she went to him before I could stop her… The only thing I could do was pull Liam clear."

Joseph hung his head, his body sagging, as he relived the moment that Alexa had broken free of him. She'd thrown herself directly into the path of the exploding microwaves, her body's own energy adding to the surge of power.

Sebastian reached out a hand towards him. His fingers gripped the younger man's shoulder. Mara knew that he felt the loss of Ross and Alexa deeply, but he didn't blame *this* man.

"There is nothing for you to feel guilty about, Joseph. The child is safe and her parents are together, as they should be. You know that they are not really gone, that they will soon be back with us, in their natural forms."

Joseph nodded, but his eyes still held remorse.

For several moments Sebastian stared at him in silent understanding. When he spoke, his voice and expression were uncompromising, "There is only one person responsible for what happened today. Mr. Cameron, a man we need to look at closely. A man we have to find at all costs. He is the person that I hold accountable, for ripping a family apart, for the deaths of those human men. Without Mr. Cameron, none of this would have happened."

Joseph nodded again, with slightly more vigour. A moment later he was hustled away from them. A group of Lifelights pulled him over to an even larger gathering. They wanted his first-hand account of what had happened.

After watching them for a moment, pleased that Joseph was being welcomed to Slioch, Mara turned her attention back to Sebastian. He appeared outwardly calm, in control, but it was a façade. She recognised the storm of grief and fury swirling within him. She knew, beyond a doubt, that the events in Houston were only the beginning.

A small shiver ran along her spine.

Instinctively, she pushed herself a little closer to him, drawing his gaze. *"What is it, what aren't you telling me?"*

Sebastian's mouth curved slightly. *"Why do I bother trying to hide things from you? You've always had an uncanny knack for seeing more than I want you to."* He paused, his hand coming up to cup the side of her face, his thumb lazily tracing her cheekbone, *"I worry that this was only a minor skirmish. It was a test, to gauge how we'd react to a Lifelight being imprisoned. Those men at the offices in England, and even those in Houston, were cannon fodder. They were sacrificed by Cameron."*

"But the Lifelights did everything they could to minimise the loss of life. What makes you think he was sacrificing them? He didn't know how we'd react and he definitely didn't know about the explosion of power that Ross's death would cause. I agree that he must have suspected that Ross would eventually have to do 'something' – which could well kill Rosalyn. That's why he put them in the Faraday cage/box thing. But everything else... he couldn't have known about that."

"Couldn't he?" Sebastian asked, *"The rescue was too easy, Mara. Why didn't he send reinforcements sooner? If this was a serious attempt to capture us, there would have been more of Cameron's people there to start with. There would have been more than one holding facility, to make sure that any Lifelights attempting a rescue could be held securely once captured."*

Mara was unconvinced, *"Easy? We lost two of our people today, Sebastian; a little girl lost her parents."* She paused momentarily as something occurred to her, *"And about that... where exactly did Nathan take Rosalyn? How are you going to handle this? Rosalyn's not like me, you know. I was only three when my parents 'died' and didn't remember much about it. At eleven years old, Rosalyn will remember every detail of her ordeal and she'll definitely be aware of the Lifelights now..."*

She felt his body tense, *"You're right, of course, and it's something I've no real answer to. Never, to my knowledge, has a female Lifelight of Rosalyn's age possessed so much information about our species. It's a problem we need to acknowledge and deal with - quickly.*

"As for where Rosalyn is; the answer to that is simple. She's still in Texas, safe with Nathan. He's taken her to the hill country, where she can be better protected."

Mara felt relieved, knowing that the young girl was being cared for, *"So, she's safe for now. We still need to make some decisions though, about how much knowledge she has about us. We have both British and American Lifelights present in Slioch. Perhaps now would be a good time to talk about this? You could call more of your family here if you wished and then, surely, we could work something out."*

He was nodding, before she'd finished speaking. *"You're right. There are enough Lifelights present to vote on this. The American Lifelights, Rosalyn's family, will abide by whatever is decided here. The fact that Joseph, Liam and I are also present will add validity to whatever is agreed on."*

Politics in action, Mara thought, *even Lifelights aren't immune to it.*

Sebastian raised his hand towards Marcus.

Her parents moved across to them immediately, their eyes mirror images of concern.

Marcus was the first to speak, "You're worried about Rosalyn?" His voice was quiet and grave but still held the power that Mara had come to expect from him.

Both of them nodded. She felt Sebastian tighten his hold on her. It was a reflexive action, one she took comfort from.

"Yes." He agreed, "This is a new situation for the Lifelights and it's important that we deal with it as soon as possible. How much information should we give the child? We have the power to make her memories fade or even take them away altogether, but we must be sure that whatever we do, it's the right thing for Rosalyn. She's been through a terrible ordeal, is now in a place she's never been to before, and she's lost her parents. We must be careful not to distress or confuse her further."

Marcus nodded in agreement. For a moment his eyes dipped to the floor of the cave, and he frowned. Then he turned on the spot and walked across to a large slab of stone positioned, like an altar, in the centre of the main cavern. It was circular in shape, its surface sparkling in the light cast by more than a dozen candles arranged around its outer edge.

With a leap, he landed in the centre of the rock, the movement drawing the attention of every Lifelight in the cavern. Silence fell.

Marcus's voice was solemnity itself, "Your attention, please.

"As you are aware, today has been a time of loss. Human lives, destroyed by the terrible events in

Houston, can never be reclaimed. It was a senseless waste that will remain with us forever.

"Ross and Alexa Munroe, parents to Rosalyn, have entered the next phase of their cycle. The volume of energy that Ross was forced to contain, proved too much for him. The ensuing explosion was so violent that neither he, nor his wife, had enough energy left to regenerate their human forms. They had no option but to return to their natural state.

"Make no mistake; their deaths in human terms were nothing short of murder. It seems that we've entered a time of extreme danger for our species, a war between us and an uncertain enemy.

"There have been casualties in this war already, on both sides. But however shocked we are by the violence, we must make sure that a victim of that violence, a child, is not overlooked.

"You should know that our enemies tried to control our family members, Ross and Alexa, through their daughter. They were prepared for her to die in order to get what they wanted. Rosalyn is only eleven years old and she has already suffered extreme trauma. The question is; how do we help her to cope with it? Do we allow her to retain what she already knows about her parents and the Lifelights or do we fade those memories, perhaps take them away altogether?

"We must vote on this matter as soon as possible, but first, is there anyone present who feels that they have something to say that may be relevant to the final decision?" Marcus stopped speaking to let his eyes wander across the Lifelights gathered around him.

After a moment's hesitation a husky, masculine voice spoke up, "I believe that I have something to say, that should be taken into consideration."

Turning, Mara saw that it was the Lifelight who'd helped Ross, Liam, who'd stepped forward. He looked ill at ease to be the focus of attention, but equally determined. "There is something that happened, when Nathan and I entered the Faraday cage." He paused, as if trying to think of the best way to phrase what he wanted to say.

Marcus looked down at him with understanding, "Take your time, Liam, you know better than most what happened in Houston and you are the only one here that was in that cage. What is it that bothers you?"

Liam frowned, as if what he was about to say confused him, "She said his name."

Mara, still held close to Sebastian, felt him stiffen and looked up at him questioningly, but he was staring at Liam. His eyes sparked.

A moment later, Marcus asked the question that Mara desperately wanted to hear the answer to, "Whose name, Liam?"

"Nathan's; Rosalyn said Nathan's name. It was as if she knew him, though I know for a fact that neither of us had met her before. Ross and Alexa were careful to keep her unaware of the Lifelights." Liam sighed, "It makes no sense to me, but I know what I heard. The moment that Nathan stepped into that cage, Rosalyn knew who he was. She didn't even struggle when he picked her up, she just clung to him. Then she passed out."

No one spoke for several long moments, until Mara finally cleared her throat. Still looking at Sebastian, she allowed herself a small, knowing smile, "So, it isn't as rare as you thought?"

For his part, Sebastian seemed incapable of speech. It was left to Marcus to ask, "What are you talking about, Mara?"

Stepping forward, Mara went to stand by Liam before turning to smile up at her father, "What Liam has just described makes me believe that Nathan was the best possible person to rescue Rosalyn. I know you all believe that Lifelights find their partners again when the women's gifts begin to return, but it would seem that isn't always the case." She looked across at Sebastian, "Severe mental trauma seems to be capable of creating a temporary link… to the one person who can bring comfort. Ask Sebastian what age I was when he first knew of me; I think the answer will surprise you."

Sebastian didn't wait for Marcus to ask the question, his voice clear and steady as he gave the answer, "Mara was only three when I first felt her presence. On the morning that she was told of your death, she connected with me. It was only the briefest of touches, but I knew immediately where she was and what had happened. Then it was gone, but I knew that she was safe and that the Lifelights had already gone to her. I don't even think that Mara was aware of what her mind had done."

Marcus nodded, as if he was aware that such a thing was possible. His words confirmed it a moment later, "Yes, I've heard of this before. However, knowing how to briefly connect with your partner, in a moment of need, is a little different to knowing his or her name and accepting their presence as natural."

Shrugging, Sebastian crossed over to Mara and put his arm around her shoulders, before giving his opinion, "Rosalyn had witnessed what was happening to her father. It's possible that the experience made her more open to the connection with Nathan made it stronger. No one knows what passed between father and daughter whilst they were held in the Faraday cage. It's possible that Ross realised that he wasn't going to survive and tried to prepare Rosalyn for what was about to happen."

Thoughtfully, Marcus rubbed at his beard, his eyes resting first on Liam and then Mara and Sebastian, "I'd say that's a distinct possibility. It's what I'd have done. Ross would, at the very least, have needed to explain why Rosalyn couldn't be near him. It would have been natural for her to seek comfort from him, but physical contact, a hug, would have been out of the question. If that was the case, she could well have been feeling confused about what she was being told, what she was seeing. A connection with her partner would be something her subconscious would crave. I still find it incredible that Nathan was there though. It's too much of a coincidence that he, her partner, would be the one to rescue her."

Sebastian shook his head at this, "Not such a coincidence, if you consider that Nathan volunteered to train with me, for a scenario just like the one in Houston. I've been readying my own mini army. For a while now, I've been convinced that the energy industry was poised to make their move on us. Nathan was good at his job. It didn't occur to me to question his enthusiasm.

"Who knows? Perhaps he was aware of Rosalyn long before she and Ross were taken? You know as well as I do that finding our partners within each cycle is not an exact science."

"So where do we go from here?" Mara knew what it was like to lose her parents and she also knew that there was a lot that she'd been grateful for in her childhood. She wanted Rosalyn to have the same advantages that she had, "Think about it, I was aware of the Lifelights long before I knew their connection to me. Their presence soothed me and comforted me every bit as much as my grandparents did. Personally, I think Rosalyn is capable of handling far more information than me. I'm not saying that Nathan, if he is her partner, should reveal who he is. I just don't see why it shouldn't be him that helps her deal with everything that's already happened…" She allowed her voice to trail off, hoping that she'd said enough. She didn't agree with the idea of removing Rosalyn's memories.

"Should we leave her with the full horror of it then?" Marcus asked, staring at her. He looked proud that she'd spoken up.

Mara shook her head, "No, not the *full* horror of it, just enough to give her an awareness that there is more to this world than meets the eye, both good and bad. She'll need to find a niche for herself, a life she can be comfortable with. She'll also need the support of everyone around her, whether they're human or Lifelight."

Silence reigned for several moments, and then the murmuring began as the Lifelights discussed what they'd heard.

Having let the pockets of discussion continue for several minutes, Marcus raised his hand towards the cavern's ceiling, calling back their attention. "So, we shall vote then; all those in favour of taking the horror completely from Rosalyn's life, please raise your hands."

About a third of those present at the cavern responded. Nodding, Marcus spoke again, "And now, all those in favour of leaving her with all of her memories intact?" Again hands were raised.

"And, how many of you feel it's wise to dim the child's memories?"

Raising her hand and feeling Sebastian do the same beside her; Mara glanced round to see that this suggestion had the most support. Relaxing slightly, she was surprised when Marcus voiced a fourth question, "And finally, how many of you agree that, if he is her partner, Nathan should be allowed to stay with Rosalyn – to protect her?"

The largest proportion of hands was raised and Mara felt a surge of joy as she watched. Rosalyn would be cared for. She would grieve for the parents she'd lost, but she would also be surrounded by love, nurtured.

She knew that all Lifelights took the defence of their families seriously. Rosalyn would be cared for by the American Lifelights, but her extended family stretched worldwide.

Turning to Sebastian, she reached up to draw his head down to hers, wanting to share the relief and joy that she felt in that moment. If Rosalyn could one day feel as strongly for Nathan as she did about Sebastian, then her future would be a happy one.

She was shocked when he pushed her away. She was even more so, when she heard the words that slid across her mind.

"Enough, my love, you're driving me insane. Emotions are running high, and I haven't forgotten that we've only fused once in this cycle.

"I think it's time that I spoke to your father."

"What?!" She stared in consternation as Sebastian walked away from her, across to where Marcus was still standing in the centre of the altar. Her father's arms were crossed, his head tilted to one side as he watched Sebastian approach and… he was smiling.

Dread settled heavily on her shoulders as she watched that same smile broaden, as Sebastian spoke to him. She caught snippets of the conversation through their link.

Her chin dropped to her chest in defeat, her body drooping with resignation, *"Oh no, not that again!"* She thought. *For goodness sake, the Lifelights are an immortal species that take only one partner, for the duration of their existence. So why on earth do they have this fixation with weddings?*

"Behave yourself, my Mara."

"Go take a running jump, Sebastian. I don't want to do this today."

"Don't look so dejected, Mara."

The feminine voice, right beside her, made her jump, "You've just survived the worst day in Lifelight history, not to mention influencing an important vote with regard to Rosalyn."

Turning her head, Mara saw a group of female Lifelights. At the front of them, and the woman who had spoken, was Rebecca Austin.

"I'm not dejected; I'm just trying to figure out how I can avoid what I *think* is heading my way."

Rebecca laughed, "You mean your wedding?"

"Yeah, that would be it." Mara groaned.

"But why? Don't you think that you and everyone else deserve something happy to focus on? This has been a sad day for all of us, but there's a time for everything. It's time to celebrate the continuity of our species, the power of the cycles and the wonder of finding our partners."

Rebecca's argument was persuasive, but Mara couldn't help thinking that the reasons behind the marriage ceremony weren't quite so high minded as that… there was something teasing at her mind, a memory that she couldn't quite pin down.

"Is that really why this ceremony is so important?" She asked.

Rebecca grinned, as the other Lifelights began to giggle, "No… let's just say, pay-back's a bitch."

CHAPTER 20

Rebecca laughed at Mara's obvious confusion.

"Let me explain." She murmured, leaning over to whisper in her ear, "Every cycle we women go through the first change. When our partners find us and our memories and talents begin to return, we're thrown into the mother of all learning curves. That happens. Every. Single. Time."

"So?" Mara asked, still not understanding.

"So, *we* decided that really wasn't fair. The men get to enjoy their memories and powers all the way through their lives. It's only right that we get to do something extra special in return…" Rebecca pointed out.

"Yes, but don't forget that those same men have to go through puberty knowing that their partners are out there and not being able to do a thing about it… that's got to hurt." Mara pointed out.

Rebecca looked horrified, "Ssshhh! Don't go saying things like that… it took us ages to get them to agree to this, without you throwing a spanner in the works now!"

"But…"

It was Mara's grandmother that spoke next, "No 'buts' my girl. We negotiated a once a cycle deal with the men. We get a wedding, a new dress, romance, the full works. Every. Single. Cycle. They don't particularly like it, but we *love* it. What woman wouldn't?"

"Me." Mara huffed, "I *hate* being the centre of attention."

"Yes, we know, you've mentioned that." Rebecca confessed. They'd obviously had this discussion before, "Tough. This is tradition. *Our* tradition. Your father won't be happy until he's officiated at the ceremony and I happen to *love* playing at being mother of the bride." She tugged at her daughter's hand, "So come on… we have work to do."

Mara didn't budge.

"Would it help if I told you that straight after the ceremony, you and Sebastian get to head off for a honeymoon?" Rebecca cajoled, "Just think of that… time alone. Time to…"

"Fuse." Sebastian whispered. His wicked chuckle teased her mind.

Mara cringed. No way was she going to have that conversation with her mother. Especially not with an audience, "Okay, I get the message. I'm up for it."

"I thought that was Sebastian's job…"

"Mum!"

* * * *

As if in a dream, Mara found herself being escorted into one of the smaller caves, where she was undressed and gently coaxed into a simple shift of midnight blue. The fluid fabric was coated in a film of shimmering energy. It looked and felt different to anything Mara had experienced so far.

The women called the energy Lancite, explaining that it held a deep significance for all Lifelights and always formed part of their marriage or bonding ceremonies. It caused the fabric of the gown to twinkle with particles of silver and gold, as if stars and planets had been scattered across its surface.

Mara's hair was then artfully arranged in a complex array of curls. They cascaded down her back in a river of black, with yet more Lancite applied to them, so that light winked out from deep within the strands. As a final touch, though she had no idea how they came to have it, the birthday gift that Jennie had given her, the necklace of sparkling blue beads, was placed around her neck.

Mara was silent throughout, her mind filled with so many sensations. The ability to speak was as unattainable as her ability to comprehend how all this could be happening to her in the first place.

At last, satisfied, the women surrounded her as Rebecca took Mara's hands and guided her back out into the main cavern.

The stone columns, the carved and painted walls, the hundreds of candles and the Lapis Lazuli sky… everything glittered. Especially the gemstone constellations, embedded in the ceiling above.

Looking across to the centre altar, ringed with candles, Mara's eyes locked with Sebastian's.

Everything else faded into the background of her vision. Her mind was besieged by a wave of love and desire that took her breath away. The undiluted joy, that she'd only ever felt in his presence, returned with a vengeance.

She forgot to be frightened by an uncertain future.

She forgot to be embarrassed.

She forgot they had an audience.

She forgot to be annoyed with her interfering parents.

As Mara crossed to take Sebastian's hand, she knew beyond a shadow of a doubt that this was what she'd been born for.

Soon, they'd go to Rosalyn. They'd make sure that she was safe and well, make plans for her future and start the search for their enemies.

But for now, she needed to give herself wholly to the one Lifelight who understood and loved her. Her…

unexciting, attention averse, awkward, different, passionate, gloriously happy, Mara Austin.

Sebastian Oran.

EPILOGUE

One Year Later...

No one noticed the couple as they appeared together on the hillside. Thunder and lightning crashed spectacularly overhead, illuminating the sky with ribbons of light. The air trembled.

Seeming not to feel the rain that slanted across them, the couple began to make their way, hand in hand, towards the house that was nestled at the foot of the hillside. Its lights welcomed them, against the dark backdrop of the storm.

"They won't be expecting us. Are you sure this is fair?"

The smooth masculine voice was in direct contrast to the light, feminine one that replied.

"Perhaps you're right. It's not fair to pay unexpected visits; but it is definitely fun! I can't wait to see their faces!"

A few minutes later, they'd reached the edge of an empty corral. The man vaulted the fence with an economy of effort. He reached out to catch the woman, as she launched herself at him from the top rail.

Looking down at her, cradled in his arms, he laughed. *"It never fails to surprise me, how easily you've embraced this life. It's hard to believe that I found you only a year ago.*

"Tell me again, why we didn't arrive on the porch, dry, instead of walking through a storm like this?"

Grinning up at him, the woman linked her arms around his neck and allowed herself to be carried the rest of the way, *"Because I wanted to feel the electricity in the air and the wetness of the rain against my skin. It gives me a buzz."*

"Hmm, well, I can certainly appreciate the buzz of the storm, but the wetness of rain? You're mad."

"Probably," she agreed, unconcerned that she was soaking wet. When they reached the door of the ranch house, she pulled on the doorbell hanging beside them.

As they waited for the door to be opened, she squinted over his shoulder at the countryside that surrounded them. She loved the Texas hill country, with its combination of rolling landscape, scrub land and lush wooded areas. It was a place of contrasts and wide open spaces - somewhere she felt happy.

Of course, that happiness could have something to do with the people who lived here… especially the person who pulled open the front door to stare at them in consternation through the screening. There was a stunned pause, before the screen door was shoved aside with a scream of delight.

"Mara, Sebastian! Why didn't you tell us you were coming?!" Jennie pulled them quickly inside, "Look at you. You're soaked!"

"Mara wanted to experience the storm – especially the 'wetness of rain'" Sebastian explained patiently, exchanging a knowing look with Jennie as he slid Mara down to the floor.

"Typical." Jennie laughed, just as Paul came into view carrying a stack of towels and blankets, "Come on, let's get you by the fire, before you catch your deaths."

Mara grinned at that, allowing her friend to tow her into the living room, "Hardly likely."

Jennie wrinkled her nose, "No, I suppose not. Don't suppose you saw Rosa as you came in, did you?"

"No, isn't she here?" Mara felt the first stirrings of disappointment at the thought that they'd missed their favourite girl, Rosalyn (Rosa for short).

Paul, now busy in the kitchen making coffee, leaned through the door to put her mind at rest. "Oh, she just slipped out to the stables to see Kim and family. Nathan was heading that way too, last I saw of him."

"Kim?" Mara and Sebastian both looked puzzled, making Paul laugh.

"Oh, of course, Kim wasn't with us the last time you visited, was she? Well, Kim is short for 'Kimberley Kitten Cat' – please don't ask me to explain the name. It was Rosa's choice. Anyway, she's just had a litter of kittens. With any luck, they'll be good mouse catchers. Although, the way Rosa spoils them, I'm not holding out much hope for that one." Paul disappeared again, only to reappear a moment later, complete with a tray filled with steaming mugs of coffee and a plate of Jennie's home-baked cookies.

Curling up on one of the large, comfy sofas that dominated the main living area, Mara settled herself back with a sigh of contentment. The towels and blankets were still sitting in a neat pile on the table next to her, unused, although Mara and Sebastian were perfectly dry now. They showed no sign that they'd been out in the storm.

Glancing from the towels to her bone dry guests, Jennie laughed, "I don't think I'll ever get used to that, the fact that you two don't operate like the rest of us. I suppose you manipulated the heat from the fire to get yourselves dry so quick?"

Sebastian grinned, "Something like that. It seemed a shame to mess up your nice clean linens, Jennie."

"Much appreciated," Jennie said, grinning back, "Laundry duty isn't top of my list of 'fun things to do'."

Mara bent forward and picked up one of the mugs of coffee and a cookie, enjoying the bitter taste of the hot fluid as it slid across her tongue before allowing the sweetness of the cookie to chase it away. She sighed with pleasure. There really was a lot to be said for home baking; it was a pity that she didn't have more time for it these days. "So, how are things with you, Rosa and Nathan?"

Jennie shrugged, taking a seat on the sofa opposite to the one Mara and Sebastian occupied. When Paul joined her, she slid her hand into his and her face took on the slightly 'soppy' look she always wore when her husband was around. They'd married nine months ago.

"Oh, everything's great. The Obermeiers, next door, have been wonderful. They helped us to settle in, and Paul's new job is working out well. Of course, if it wasn't for Nathan and the other guys, we'd struggle with the land that's attached to this place, but so far so good."

Sebastian helped himself to his second cookie, "No thoughts on opening 'The Tea Cosy' mark two then?"

Jennie shook her head, laughing, "Nah, too busy looking after the house and Rosa. She's making friends, slowly, but I still like to be around as much as I can for her. I take this whole 'guardian' thing seriously, you know..."

As if on cue, the back door clattered open and laughter and voices could be heard coming from the kitchen. A moment or two later a young man and a girl came into view. There was another stunned silence.

The girl, slim built with a mass of blonde hair and dark brown eyes, reminiscent of her mother, Alexa, stopped and stared for a moment. Then she launched herself at the couple who'd stood up to greet her.

"Auntie Mara, Uncle Sebastian! I didn't know you were coming to visit!"

Rosalyn's voice had risen to a scream of excitement as she wrapped her arms around them.

Her enthusiasm was infectious. Picking her up, Sebastian twirled her round, narrowly missing the tray of coffee. Laughing, he set her down again, "Happy to see us, little one?" He asked, tugging at her hair affectionately.

Rosa pushed him and Mara back down onto the sofa, and then plonked herself between the two of them, "Yep! How long are you staying this time?"

Mara smiled, "Oh, only a couple of days, I'm afraid. We'll make sure they count though." She glanced up, smiling at the young man, who was looking like he very much wanted to turn and run. "It's nice to see you again, Nathan, still keeping you busy here?"

Nathan was tall and still a little gangly looking, even at twenty three. With the sort of work he was doing on the land though, he was starting to develop some serious muscles. His hair, worn longer than some would approve of, was dark gold in colour, similar to Paul's. His eyes, set in a tanned, handsome face, were a fascinating shade of green; dark and mysterious looking. All in all, he was an attractive looking man, and Mara hadn't been surprised to see the look of adoration in Rosa's eyes as they walked into the living room. It would seem that she had a serious crush on him.

"Yeah, they keep me busy, Mrs. Oran, but it's all good." Nathan's deep voice sounded embarrassed. He stuffed his hands in his jeans pockets and looked down at the floor.

Sebastian seemed to have noticed Rosa's hero-worship too. His eyes had narrowed slightly, as he stared at Nathan. Mara wrapped an arm around Rosa's shoulders, so that she could get her hand as near to her husband's ear as possible. Then she pinched it, hard. *"Leave it alone, Sebastian."* She warned, when he swung round to her in surprise.

Taking the hint, he smiled at Nathan and indicated the leather 'pouf' that was next to the sofa, "Why don't you join us? It's a while since we've seen you."

"Yeah, come on Nathan, take a load off – I'll get some fresh coffee on." Jennie added, not giving him a chance to refuse. She pushed him further into the room on her way through to the kitchen.

After that, the atmosphere relaxed, and the evening passed in a whirl of chatter and laughter in front of the fire.

Later that night, when everyone had gone to bed, Mara sneaked back down the stairs. In only her robe she eased through the front door and out onto the porch. Carefully navigating the creaking wooden slats, she sat herself down on the bottom step.

From here she could fully appreciate the endless, star filled sky that had followed in the wake of the storm clouds.

She didn't turn her head when she heard the door creak behind her, knowing exactly who it was well before he seated himself next to her. She almost purred, like Kimberley Kitten Cat, when he reached out to draw her close.

"It's beautiful, isn't it?" She whispered, laying her head on his shoulder.

Sebastian glanced down at her with a smile, "It is from where I'm sitting."

"I was talking about the stars, you idiot." Mara scolded.

Sebastian smiled again, reaching up to trace the side of her face and down her neck, his fingers gently teasing at the neckline of her robe, "I wasn't. How about coming for a walk with me, Mrs. Oran? I was thinking about somewhere in the hills, nice and remote, where I can have my wicked way with you."

She sighed, enjoying the warmth of his hand as it slid further into her robe, lingering on the swell of her breast. Tilting her head back, she parted her lips in silent invitation, relishing the kisses that he lavished on her mouth and face. Desire wound its way through her, heating her blood and bringing on the familiar, aching pulse that was never far away when Sebastian touched her.

"Sounds like a plan, Mr. Oran. But tell me, do they have the Northern Lights around here or are we going to be mistaken for a passing UFO this time?"

Sebastian was busy nuzzling at her neck now, but she felt his lips curve into a smile, his laughter whispering across her skin.

"Oh, a UFO, definitely, but who cares anyway?" He asked, suddenly standing and sweeping her up with him, "It's a beautiful night, the people we love are safe and well and our future at this moment looks more settled than it has for a while. Mr. Cameron may have vanished from Synergy U.S.A., but I've got people on the lookout for him and the investigation into where he came from is ongoing... because I doubt we've heard the last of him. But for now, why shouldn't we celebrate with a little light show?"

At first Mara wasn't sure how to answer. She felt her robe billow out, her laughter fading from the porch as she was carried at speed towards the surrounding hills. In the end though, it was simple.

"I can't think of anything more appealing, Sebastian, let's make it incandescent…."

The Lifelights will return in:

'Light Evolution'
Book 2 of The Lifelight Series

www.alinavoyce.com